DARK MATTER PRESENTS:

LITTLE RED FLAGS

STORIES OF CULTS, CONS, AND CONTROL

Other Books in the "Dark Matter Presents" Anthology Series

Zero Dark Thirty: The 30 Darkest Stories from Dark Matter Magazine, 2021–'22

Human Monsters: A Horror Anthology

Monstrous Futures: A Sci-Fi Horror Anthology

Monster Lairs: A Dark Fantasy Horror Anthology

The Off-Season: An Anthology of Coastal New Weird

Haunted Reels: Stories from the Minds of Professional Filmmakers

Haunted Reels 2: More Stories from the Minds of Professional Filmmakers

Edited by Noelle W. Ihli & Steph Nelson
Book Design and Layout by Rob Carroll
Cover Art by Drew Huff
Cover Design by Rob Carroll

Library of Congress Control Number: 2026932115

ISBN 978-1-958598-54-2 (paperback)
ISBN 978-1-958598-91-7 (eBook)

darkmatter-ink.com

EDITED BY

NOELLE W. IHLI & STEPH NELSON

CONTENTS

INTRODUCTION
Noelle W. Ihli & Steph Nelson 11

HONEY'S VERSION
Christopher O'Halloran 13

THE ARROW
Alex Hoeft 27

FOR I NEVER WAS SO SMALL
Marisca Pichette 37

PRODIGAL
Chris McGrane 50

UNDERFOOT
Kaleigh Rodgerson 54

RAMBUTAN
Jade Jiao 65

SIMPLE LOYALTY
J. B. McLaurin 73

SIMON SAYS
Frances Hope 84

8 • CONTENTS

MUSCLE WATER
Michael A. Reed...94

THE MOTEL CALIFORNIA
Amanda Cecelia Lang...101

YOU MADE ME WANT TO KILL THE WORLD
Catlyn Ladd...114

THUMB SUCKER
L. P. Ring..120

THE PRICE OF FAME
Nick Kolakowski...129

DEAR DANA
Sam Brackett..140

CON AND CONSEQUENCES
Jessica Lévai...147

ARKADIA
Mia Dalia..159

#IDESERVEIT
Cat Delani...167

THE GIG
Cory Swanson..175

WE CONTAIN MULTITUDES
Andrew Kozma 185

THE VESSEL
Caleb Stephens 194

TREAT DAY
J. E. Rowney 204

ABOUT THE AUTHORS 213

INTRODUCTION

NOELLE W. IHLI & STEPH NELSON

WE ALL KNOW the feeling: that subtle tightening in your gut. The flicker behind a stranger's smile. The moment the energy shifts in a conversation and you wonder, *Should I be here? Should I trust this person? Am I being paranoid?*

Most of us like to think we'd recognize danger when it comes calling. We tell ourselves we'd never fall for the slick pitch, the cotton-candy promise, the wolf in sheep's clothing. We tell ourselves we'd feel the flaxen strings tightening around our wrists.

But here's the frightening truth: Control rarely bares its teeth—not at first, anyway. It smiles. Strokes our ego. Masquerades as comfort, community, a mentor, a movement, a place to belong. And before you know it, the door to escape has softly closed behind you—and the little red flag you brushed aside.

Whether or not you've personally been caught in the snare of a cult, con, or controlling relationship, you've probably felt the first warnings. You've let someone inside your home when you wanted to ask them to leave. You've agreed to a sales pitch when you wanted to say no. You've shushed your instincts on a dark street when they whispered *run.*

Those moments are the inspiration behind this anthology.

Each story in *Little Red Flags: Stories of Cults, Cons, and Control* explores the thin line between trust and terror. In these pages, you'll find the sinister beneath the familiar, the smiling mask hiding a sneer.

We're thrilled—and a little chilled—to showcase these gripping tales from the brilliant minds of Sam Brackett,

Mia Dalia, Cat Delani, Alex Hoeft, Frances Hope, Jade Jiao, Nick Kolakowski, Andrew Kozma, Catlyn Ladd, Amanda Cecelia Lang, Jessica Levai, Chris McGrane, J. B. McLaurin, Christopher O'Halloran, Marisca Pichette, Michael A. Reed, L. P. Ring, Kaleigh Rodgerson, J. E. Rowney, Caleb Stephens, and Cory Swanson.

Their stories will draw you in with velvet gloves—and leave you wide-eyed and sleepless when you turn out the lights. You'll find stories of revenge, escape, and survival. Victims and perpetrators. Cults isolated in the forest and manipulators tucked within the walls of your own home.

So settle in, but stay sharp.

The little red flags are waving.

—Noelle & Steph

H0ney's VERSION

CHRISTOPHER O'HALLORAN

ONLY A MORON would fall in love with an animation. Only a brain-dead, tasteless child would dance alongside this pixelated nightmare. Music? Don't make me laugh. Tenth-grade poetry by the perpetually heartbroken, set to boring, repetitive, radio melodies.

Every time the Mohawks score, the crowd looks to the Jumbotron for everybody's favorite dancing celebrity, like she's the star of the show. It sets my jaw on edge every time.

"I'm getting real sick of that bitch." Dad's got his arms crossed, old Vultures scarf wrapped tightly around his frail neck. He's always colder than the rest of us. His body is fighting. "It's not bad enough they blow us out the water, we get her masked mug bouncing around every time they complete a pass."

H0ney Sparx leads the crowd in a wave. "H0ney loves you!" she squeals. The phrase that pays. The one that kicks off every one of her songs, even the sad ones. Her mask displays a scarlet, roaring lion. Its pixelated head wraps around hers entirely. The digital cover fully conceals her face.

The crowd goes wild.

Not me, though. Not Dad, coughing his disgust into the rag in his sleeve. Not the *real* fans.

They're trying to get girls into football, so H0ney Sparx is officially a representative of the Mohawks.

Vulture and Mohawk fans alike link arms and chant the bridge to one of her inane songs as it's piped over the speakers. Peace among rivals.

Kill me.

H0NEY'S "SPARKLERS" HAVE taken over social media. Her rabid fan base. Don't criticize their masked overlord; they'll doxx the shit out of you and dig up tweets from when your developing brain was the size of an apple. They'll get your ass fired.

It's H0ney's world, and we're all just living in it.

"I'm boycotting the league," says Kyle in the lunchroom. "I can't stand seeing her stupid non-face. I thought we were done with masks."

"You know we're still technically in a pandemic," says Arlene. "It's still around."

"Oh no, not the sniffles." Big Brad burps into his closed fist and loudly crumples the wrapper his triple cheeseburger came in. "They're shoving her down our throat."

"Actually," says Arlene, "I read that H0ney was only on camera for twenty-five seconds last night." She looks to the other guys in the lunchroom, but she's dreaming if she thinks she can convince us H0ney isn't taking over.

"Twenty-five seconds too many." Brad tosses his wrapper at the trash can, but it bounces off the lip and onto the ground. "Don't even get me started on those Sparklers."

"Not all H0ney fans are insane." Arlene picks up his wrapper. "Some of them are normal people. Some even work with you, jackass." She tosses the wrapper, nailing the shot, but I'm lost in my phone, scrolling through social media.

H0ney, H0ney, H0ney. It's all H0ney.

"H0ney thinks you're incredible!"

There she is, pretending to chug a bottle of syrup like it's a beer while her mask displays closed eyes and a vortex of stars within a gaping mouth.

"Just another gorgeous day with H0ney!"

In the next photo, she's hanging out with the winning Mohawks, at restaurants I'd never be able to afford. She's never seen eating. Never seen without the mask.

"H0ney says it's never too late to dream big!"

Hell, the ads are even H0ney related.

"H0ney says feeling is healing." Her face a throbbing heart. "Sign up for GOODBRAIN.COM and use the promo code ROAR15 for fifteen percent off!"

"Goddamn." I toss my phone hard onto the lunch table. All eyes on me, the boys and Arlene turning my way. "Why did I know about *H0ney's* tour before I knew about the KISS hologram tour?"

"That sounds sick," says Kyle. "I'm getting tickets for that."

I'm not here to talk about the greatest rock group of all time, though. I'm here to rage about this fake-faced bimbo.

"She's everything wrong with the world. She's so fake. There's nothing real about her. The moving mask? The screen? What the hell is that? Kids these days can't focus as is, and bullshit like that is the reason for it."

"Hell yeah, brother." Kyle raises a Coke in salute. "A bunch of us are boycotting the ugly bi—"

"Yo!" Alene intrudes. "What the fuck?"

"What?" asks Kyle. "You think she's wearing that mask 'cause she's hot? She's covering up a butterface, for sure."

"You all are disgusting." Fuming, Arlene leaves.

"Boycotts don't do shit," I mutter.

No. This requires more.

"I'm not letting them take my game from me. From—" Something catches in my throat. That Mohawks game was the last one I saw with Dad before the emphysema took him. "I won't let them."

I lock eyes with Kyle. With Big Brad.

They both nod. They're in.

IT'S EASY ENOUGH to track H0ney. Her jet has an online identifier conveniently broadcasting using real-time logs. We know when she flies into town to watch her stupid Mohawks. We know when she arrives in New York. We know when she touches down in Rome for whatever bullshit, elitist reasons popstars need to be in Rome.

Big Brad, Kyle, and I are prepared to strike as soon as the opportunity presents itself.

As soon as the alert hits our phones that H0ney has landed in Seattle again, we'll text each other the predetermined code—Bad Blood—and it's off to the races.

The plan is to steal her mask.

Smash the hell out of it.

See if the Sparklers still lose their mind for their idol when her face is exposed and she's as dumpy as they are.

H0ney won't sparkle anymore, then.

They'll never know it was us, either. After all, these days no one bats an eye at a mask.

DAYS GO BY, then weeks. She doesn't return to our rainy city. What started out as an urgent coup becomes a mind-numbing waiting game.

Eventually, Brad and Kyle and I stop talking about the plan. They bitch every Monday about how annoying H0ney was over the weekend, but I can tell their heart isn't in it when I mention the tracker.

I'm pretty sure they've turned off their alerts. During lunch, I get a ping that H0ney is in Singapore, and their phones don't even vibrate.

Resigned, I turn off alerts for H0ney's flight path.

But I check in from time to time.

I GET MY kid on alternating weekends, and this one is mine. I scrounged up enough for a couple annual passes for the zoo, so once again, that's where we go.

We sit on a bench in front of the monkeys. They watch each other, my thirteen-year-old daughter and the simians. Nobody is having a good time.

"You used to like the zoo," I grumble.

"It's all we do," she grumbles back. In her pocket, her phone chirps. A short refrain from the H0ney song, "The Darkest Shade of Red."

I wish I didn't know that. All this useless information about H0ney, filling my head.

Her hand twitches toward her phone, but with a small growl she stops herself. On the ride here, we agreed: no phones.

I scratch my elbow. A monkey copies me.

"You cool to stay here? I gotta take a leak." She can check her phone while I'm in the can. Can't say I never do anything for her.

The kid doesn't even look at me. She tosses a thumbs up my direction, though.

"Maybe after, we can do some go karts?"

"I'm meeting friends tonight."

"But it's my weekend."

She rolls her eyes at me. Apparently, that's the only response my argument warrants. I'd correct her attitude, but my bladder is fit to burst.

"We'll talk when I get back."

Once more, her thumb flicks up into the air. Cool.

I do my business in the bathroom and exit next to the concession. A snack sounds good about now, and they have a sign advertising their homemade kettle corn.

Maybe that'll turn this outing around.

The first time I gave my kid kettle corn, her eyes lit up like carnival lights. She had expected regular, salty, buttery fair popcorn. Since then, it was all she wanted when her mother and I took her out.

Before things fell apart.

I get in line behind a chick asking for a rocket pop. I'll buy my girl a treat. Remind her of how things used to be.

The girl turns. The tiny backpack she wears bumps against the counter of the concession stand, and something inside chirps a happy little tune.

"H0ney loves you!"

I freeze. There it is again. I can't escape her!

It's sad. This girl is just as obsessed as my kid. Maybe more. She's got the same haircut. Same poppy style. Looks like she even drew the same arrow-shaped mole on the back of her neck.

Only it's not drawn on. It's the real deal, elevated and textured. She stops and looks at me, rocket pop in her hand.

I didn't realize how close I got, examining the mole. Now, I'm face to face, stunned by the eyes looking into mine.

H0ney's LED mask obscures her face completely. There are no photos online of her face, but there is one of her peering out of a fully-tinted limo window. I know that photo backward and forward. Those eyes are burned into my memory.

The same eyes in front of me. Don't ask how I know, but I know. "Rocket pop," I say. "Good choice."

She tears the wrapper off the tri-colored, frozen treat and puts it in her mouth. Bites into the red top. Her silence is a challenge. She's daring me to say something.

I don't. I play it cool, despite my heart going about a million beats per minute.

Hours. I've spent hours examining this woman. Researching her, watching videos of her against my will, seeing her photos in articles the algorithm feeds me because it now thinks I'm obsessed with her.

I'm not obsessed.

She shrugs. H0ney—without her mask—shrugs and walks away.

I follow.

That hip-swinging, perky walk is ingrained in me. I've seen her walk like that down the concourse to her box at every football arena. I've seen her walk like that in the music videos I've watched over and over. Hell, I've seen her walk like that on the way to greet every talk show host on TV.

She must know I'm following; all subtlety has escaped me, and I'm trapped in the gravity of her influence. She doesn't seem to care.

When you're used to having all the power, it's hard to realize when it's totally gone.

There are no bodyguards nearby. As far as I can tell, I'm the only one who knows who this chick really is.

I can do anything. We're surrounded by people, but who's going to stop me from snatching her bag? Who's going to be a hero? Nobody does shit but film, and I can be gone by the time their camera app loads.

I stay a few feet back as she approaches the lion's enclosure and leans against the short wall that separates us from them down below. One final bite takes off the rest of her Popsicle.

I wait to see what she'll do next. It's just like a celebrity to drop the stick. Discard the trash on the ground. Someone else will pick it up, right?

But she doesn't. She places it in her pocket.

"Do you think the lions mind being watched?" she asks.

I look around. There's nobody else. Only me.

H0ney Sparx is talking to me.

"Probably not. They're always hiding." I step up to the short wall and look down into the enclosure.

There should be two lions in there, but all I can see of them is a lonely tail sticking out from an artificial cave.

"It would be kind of nice to hide like that." She looks away from the enclosure. Looks directly at me.

Kyle was dead wrong. She's not ugly.

Her dark hair is cropped at the level of her chin. Her brown eyes seem to caramelize in the light of the sun. Full lips part slightly, displaying the slightest gap between her front teeth.

Something about her is so normal, but so radiant. The blush on her cheeks. The sheen under her eyes and the slight dew under her jawline.

Makeup. Has to be. Probably has a full staff, even just for an incognito visit to the zoo. She should have had them do something about the redness in her eyes, though. She looks strung out on something.

Or like she's been crying? No. What does she have to cry about?

"They should hide," I say. "The lions. What do they have to live for? They're in a cage, where they get gawked at by idiots who stare at them through the screen of a fucking phone." I lean forward, trying to see into the cave. Nothing.

I look back at H0ney. She raises an eyebrow but doesn't reply.

"They should go back to the wild. There's no place for them here."

My words hang in the air like poison gas.

She takes a deep breath and sighs. With a slight twitch of her narrow shoulder, she shrugs out of the backpack and drops it to the ground.

Once more, whatever's inside makes a little chirp. The intro to all her songs. "H0ney loves you!" Her musical catchphrase.

"You're right," she says. Her voice is sad, quivering almost.

"Damn right, I'm right." I go back to watching the lions. I wish Brad and Kyle were here to see this. I'm pretty damn sure I've rattled her. Dropped a truth bomb on her ass.

Then she does something I don't expect.

"They should be free." H0ney darts forward and climbs on the low wall, first one leg, then another.

"What—"

I could stop her. I should stop her; this chick is only a few years older than my daughter.

But I don't. I stay right where I am, watching as she slips over the edge and falls to the ground, twenty feet below.

There's a crack. A small cry.

"Jesus," I mutter. I look over the edge and she's on the ground. Her ankle is already swelling. Broken for sure.

I want to yell at her to run, but I don't want to alert the lions. They haven't noticed her.

Yet.

"Get out of there," I stage whisper, starting to panic. This isn't what I wanted.

She doesn't listen. On a wounded ankle, she rises and begins to limp toward the tail hanging lazily out of the cave.

I pick up her backpack. It's all I can think to do.

She steps up to the cave and peers inside. She doesn't look at me. She only has eyes for the lions.

When she reaches down and pulls the tail, I look away. I don't want to see.

But I can't help hearing. I squeeze the bag tight.

Inside, the mask makes its chirp, but I can barely hear it. Not over the screaming.

"WHAT ARE THE sirens for?" asks my daughter, her eyes wide. She's out of breath from the run for the parking lot beneath the automated announcement telling us that the zoo is now closing. "Was there a bomb threat or something?"

"Accident." I wipe sweat out of my eyes. The AC in my van is busted, but I don't want to roll the windows down. Don't want to draw attention to myself. I know it's crazy. No one will be looking for me, but the police will have questions for the last person to see H0ney alive.

And they'll know that was me. Because I'm in possession of stolen property; H0ney's mask is under my seat in the bag I took. I haven't had the chance to look inside the bag, but I could feel it pressing against my gut when I hid it under my shirt.

"Oh shit. I'm looking it up." My daughter peers even closer at her phone, nose nearly touching the screen.

God help me if she finds out the truth in this van. She's a diehard Sparkler. Her obsession doesn't stop with that annoying ringtone. Her stepdad got her three of H0ney's albums in vinyl last year, despite them not even owning a record player. She even made a post about it. Couldn't be bothered to say anything about the Sephora gift card I got her off her mom's advice, but that's fine.

"I doubt there will be any news about it. Not this quick."

She looks up at me like she just found out Santa isn't real. "H0ney was there?"

"Get off your phone."

"Turn around," she says. "Was she supposed to be at the zoo?" She's back on her phone, frantically scrolling and typing, searching her Insta, her TikTok. Her eyes are huge. Obsessed. Elsewhere. "This can't be true. No, no, no, this…"

She finds the news.

"She's dead," whispers my daughter. "TMZ leaked it."

I didn't do shit. I didn't kill her, so why am I shaking like I did? I chance a look to my side.

Her face is completely still—no trembling lip, no crinkled forehead like when she was a kid. But the tears fall freely, running down her cheeks and off her chin, onto the phone screen.

"Turn around, Daddy."

It hurts to be called Daddy again. It's all I've wanted for years, but right now, it's a knife in my guts.

"No."

"Daddy, please." She turns to me, grabbing my forearm. "I need to be close to her. I need to be there!"

"I said no." I shake her off. "Don't touch me while I'm driving. You want to kill us?"

My kid gives me a hurt look I see out the corner of my eyes. Crying, but I can feel the anger radiating off her face.

She doesn't want to kill us, but right now, she wants to kill *me*.

I grip the steering wheel tighter and focus on the road. It's only temporary. She'll get over it.

Maybe someday, when she's older, I'll give her that mask under the seat. Tell her I bought it off eBay.

The last remaining piece of H0ney Sparx.

THE BOYS ARE riled up once more.

They don't want me to keep the mask hidden under my bed. That'd be a waste of a golden opportunity. They have grander plans.

My daughter won't be getting the mask after all. Probably for the best.

"Light it on fire," says Big Brad. "Let's watch the LEDs explode."

"You're thinking too small," says Kyle, thick nails stroking a dull-brown goatee. It's new. A little post-divorce addition. "We need to send a message."

I nod, but I keep flashing back to those screams I heard from the lion enclosure. I've had dreams about it ever since.

"So," says Brad, flicking the wheel of a Bic lighter adorned with a bikini babe. "We film us lighting it on fire?"

In my man cave, us three surrounding the chair on which I've propped the mask, I shake my head.

Kyle speaks before I find my voice. Slowly, so he knows we're watching. Paying close attention.

"I know exactly what we should do."

WE DISGUISE OURSELVES using the COVID masks my ex left behind when she fell for the CDC's brainwashing. Kyle claims it's too hard to breathe in his, so he runs the camera, face and goatee out of the limelight.

Our demands are simple: Keep the cameras on the players. Ban celebrities from attending the games. Remove quarterback protections and bring back the toughness that made it worth watching.

Do all that, and we'll return H0ney's mask.

Her death can bring some good. Not to the Sparklers, but to us. The sports fans who just wanted to be left the fuck alone.

It doesn't matter how sad she was. What did she have to be sad about? She was bad for society. Bad for our game.

Bad for my little girl.

If I keep telling myself this, I can almost forget the sounds of her in the lion's den. Almost.

"How do we know this is really H0ney's mask?" asks Big Brad, turning to me. "How did you know that chick was actually her and not some deranged Sparkler with a knock-off?"

H0ney's mask looks back at us from the folding chair where Kyle duct taped it. Not that it could walk out of here without a face to ride out, but the visuals need to be right. Duct tape shows we're not fucking around.

The video we posted from an anonymous account already has 20,000 views. That number is exploding in real time.

TikTok, reels, shorts. It's everywhere, and everyone is watching it.

Kyle disabled the comments. Spare us the whining.

"It's the real one," I say. "Read the fucking news. They know it's missing."

"Uh, guys." Kyle's eyes are glued to his phone. "I think they found us."

The temperature in my man cave drops ten degrees.

"Who?" I ask. "The…the police?"

"Worse." Kyle says. He holds out his phone. "Sparklers."

I grab his phone. The Pop socket yanks on his finger, and Kyle lets out a squeal.

"Pussy." I scroll through his phone, my finger slipping on the screen. Why am I sweating so goddamn much? There's no way they found us. There's nothing in the video that indicates where we are.

Or so I thought.

I read through the comments on a Reddit thread, blood pounding in my ears.

These fanatics—these freaks—they saw two airplanes pass through the slice of sky in the little window in my man cave. They triangulated the times and the flight logs using the same app I used to track H0ney's jet. So, they know we're in Seattle.

They searched real estate listings for houses containing a basement. Houses built before a certain year as well, since my windows haven't been up to recent energy-efficient codes.

The timestamps on all these Reddit comments show it took them less than twenty minutes to pinpoint my address.

Faintly, from upstairs, the doorbell rings.

My heart jumps. I tell myself I'm not shaking. That's just low blood sugar. I'm not scared of a bunch of teenage girls and soccer moms.

"We need to leave," I say. "Side door."

Brad groans.

"What?" I snap.

Brad's face sinks in horror. He's looking at the narrow awning window up by the basement ceiling. The one that gave us away.

Faces peer in. Angry eyes behind pointing fingers.

Homemade masks made of paper plates are tied to their faces. They all read *JUSTICE FOR H0NEY*, scrawled from ear to ear.

A sea of blonde-highlighted hair frames the bulk of the blank masks. Behind the paper plates, teeth gnash.

They've spotted H0ney's mask, duct-taped to the chair. All bets are off.

Wood cracks upstairs. Must be the door; footsteps pound above our heads.

"Cut the mask loose," says Kyle. "Give it back to them!"

"It's too late." I'm shaking. My hands, my knees. It's a miracle I'm even standing.

The door to my man cave flies open. The masked Sparklers swarm in.

Kyle's the first to scream. They have him on the ground, restraining him like he's a wild animal. Their arms are pistons, cycling in and out of the melee with mechanical speed and regularity. Punching, scratching, kicking, tearing.

All I see of Kyle is a brief splash of red. A tooth sliding across the laminate floor to rest at the leg of the chair holding H0ney's mask.

Brad holds his lighter to the thing. "Don't touch me!" he screams, and flicks the ignition wheel, but he's shaking too much to get a proper flame. "I'll do it! Don't touch me!"

They're too far gone to lend his threat any credence. The Sparklers swarm him, too. A wave of round, white faces like giant two-dimensional pearls.

They rip the lighter from Brad's mitts and throw him into the BowFlex in the corner of my man cave. Slammed against the heavy weights. Shoved into the rod system.

Hands grab me. Small, sharp hands. On their wrists, handmade bracelets proclaim their love for H0ney and friendship.

"No," I moan. "Please. I'm sorry."

I'm surrounded by paper faces. Mouths scream through gaping holes cut in the plates.

They pull. My arms stretch. My legs.

Something pops in my knee and a white-hot heat flares up my leg.

Then more heat from elsewhere. One of the girls found Brad's lighter. Flames chew up the curtains on either end of the basement window. Smoke begins to fill the room, burning my nose.

I scream, but my face is full of light.

H0ney's mask presses against my face, but someone else is wearing it. A young woman with straight, blonde hair poking out the bottom of the full mask. Close to the same age as my kid, if I had to guess.

Was my daughter one of those Reddit commenters? Did she help these women find me? Is she in this crowd, behind a homemade paper mask, watching them tear me limb from limb?

The blonde girl speaks, and H0ney's mouth moves. The mouth of the devil.

Angry light pours out of its eyes, bright led white shooting flares of pain through my head.

I can't hear. The pain is too loud. The flames are too loud.

I just wanted my game back. I just wanted my daughter back.

Another pop in my shoulder. They're tearing me apart.

The young woman leans closer.

H0ney leans closer. The new H0ney. Her voice is high and giddy.

"Look what you made us do."

THE ARROW

ALEX HOEFT

WEEDS PUSHED UP through the concrete, splitting wide the cracks.

Ellen stood, hands on hips, admiring the take-back—the exacted revenge. Mankind didn't grow roots, but Mother Nature did. And she didn't let things lie, not out here where humans rarely ventured.

DSLR hanging around her neck, Ellen lifted a hand to shield her eyes and looked east, following the trajectory she'd started in San Francisco. Before her lay the southeast corner of Wyoming.

Coordinates saved in the handheld GPS clipped to her belt, Ellen shrugged on her daypack and turned back for her van, parked next to a ravine a few miles away. She would spend the evening hunched over her makeshift desk, poring over satellite imagery to find the next location. The consistency helped; there were about ten to fifteen miles between each point. And, of course, one marker always pointed to the next.

Ellen had found just over a hundred markers so far. And however many there were to go, she would find their end.

FOR THE PAST year, Ellen had spent most of her time alone, on the road. When she did cross paths with the odd stranger, she could always tell the exact moment they regretted striking up a conversation. The polite shine of intrigue in their eyes dulled, like curtains being drawn.

Her opener, at least, seemed to hit the mark. Leaning over—in line at the grocery store, across the counter at a coffee shop, she'd say, "I'm on a quest."

That usually earned a double take, a lift of eyebrows. "Oh?" they'd say with a wry smile. "A quest, huh?"

Ellen would nod, hands coming up to help paint the picture. Imagine this: Giant concrete arrows, built atop the land like a dispersed sidewalk. Twenty feet long. Isolated locations, pointing out an eastern trail across the country. There could be hundreds.

The other person would lean forward and ask, "Where do they lead, do you think?" Sometimes, there'd be a joke. "Buried treasure?"

Ellen would mirror her newest confidant's eagerness. "A government test site is my theory," she'd say. "Completely off-grid."

And just like that, down came the shutters. They would sit back, even turn away, muttering a faint "good luck" or sometimes nothing at all.

Likely, it was her audience. Twenty-year-old baristas in cities she was passing through, too obsessed with the latest memes to care about long-hidden government secrets or a subtly crafted plot. Or, in the sleepy mountain or farm towns, gas station attendants too jaded to bother with yet another over-excited tourist.

Ellen wanted to grab them by the shoulders. *How can you not care?!* she imagined asking. *A connection of dots across the very belly of the country. Forgotten! Ignored! They're leading to something and we're just sitting here, going about our lives!*

She had multiple working theories as to what lay at the end of the path of arrows: a deep state headquarters, perhaps; a CIA black site; or the most complex surveillance operation in the world. All of the above, even.

There was only one man who hadn't turned away from the conversation. Back at a bar in middle-of-nowhere Nevada. He'd perked up at her suggestion of government malfeasance, and Ellen thought, *yes.* So close to Area 51, of course these people would understand.

But no. "That's an old transcontinental airmail route," he said, legs spread wide. "Built back in the 1920s and '30s, guiding pilots across the country, all the way to the East Coast. Used to have beacon towers on top of 'em."

"And no one ever did anything with the arrows, all these years later?" Ellen countered. "Society advanced and they left the slabs of concrete there to rot?"

"Nothing more than relics," the man said with a shrug.

He was a fool. Ellen knew the trail would lead to something bigger. Airmail! Ha! At one point the arrows might have been used for that purpose, perhaps, she amended privately. But a century later? Coordinates forgotten by everyone. Except the people who wanted them forgotten.

Except Ellen, who, since happening upon the first arrow while out mapping cell towers, quickly realized that if she didn't commit to following the path to its end, no one would.

ANOTHER ARROW: 41.181378, -104.503735

And another, farther east: 41.214164, -103.252222

Ellen drove and parked and hiked and recorded coordinates. She posted her progress to her blog, *Quest for Truth*, faithfully read by a small but growing readership drawn from corners of the Internet not so inclined to blindly trust mainstream media. Some of them even donated money for gas and food. The generosity was unnecessary, with Ellen's savings from three decades as a meter reader, yet the financial support on top of their comments and shares was encouraging.

They don't want us to know, Ellen wrote in one of her daily updates. *They leave a trail of breadcrumbs and think because it's so far removed from society, we won't follow.*

She drove, parked, hiked, and recorded coordinates. "I'm getting closer," she'd say, standing at the center of each arrow. At night, she'd stretch out on the bed in the back of her van and dream of what awaited.

I'm certain these arrows lead to something, she wrote in another post. *Something they don't want us to find. Whatever's at the end, I swear to share the truth. I'll pull back the wool over our eyes.*

Ellen was a self-taught cartographer, an amateur using rulers and compasses on her maps, or scrolling carefully across Google Earth to seek out the next arrow. She assessed them one by one, researching surroundings, history, proximity to resources. What other facilities existed nearby? What were the demographics of those living closest? Trends in water supply? Primary exports? Only when she'd gathered enough information for a research paper would she turn her gaze to the next arrow.

Most had deteriorated significantly over the years, leaving only traces of concrete behind. Some took days, even weeks to find. Still, she found them. Could find them in her sleep by now, one hand behind her back and a smile on her face.

And then, in central Kansas, parked one evening outside the public library for its WiFi and planning her next route using satellite imagery, her smile died.

This one was all wrong.

It was as if nature had never touched the arrow: no crumbling concrete from years of exposure. The color was vivid, even through a computer screen; a bright, clear yellow. The satellite photo marked as captured only months before. The arrow appeared new; so, so new.

Most alarming was that unlike the others, this arrow didn't point east. Not even a slight variation, north- or southeast, to skirt some obstacle like a mountain range.

This arrow pointed due west.

It was a clear deviation. Ellen pulled up the coordinates again the following morning from a computer in the library, checking for consistency. Perhaps her personal computer had been hacked? An attempt to throw her off the scent? But sure enough, the public monitor showed the same, as did the one next to it.

Ellen sat back in her seat, bewildered. Then she sat forward and began a new post on her blog.

Could it be? she posed. *I've committed myself to this quest long past what anyone expected, and this is my reward: proof of deeper meaning. The point of no return. Others would have given up by now, surely, but here I still stand. Tomorrow, I will continue to seek, but I will also find. The truth is close.*

Reactions to the update encouraged Ellen. "Yes!!!" "It's as big as you've always told us!" "So weird!" "Yet more proof of government overreach, making you think you're crazy!"

Donations poured in. Ellen's heart pounded—with excitement, with terror. "I'm almost there," she said aloud, as if the two-faced politicians strong-arming this country could hear her.

UP CLOSE, THE arrow took her breath away.

Not a single mark on the surface, the color so bright under the afternoon sun it was nearly blinding. The lines and angles were sharp, like the concrete had been poured just the day prior. She felt a sudden, odd aversion to standing on it.

Ellen took in her surroundings. They were the same as they'd been the entire eight-mile hike in: rolling hills of grass rippling in the breeze. Woods to her left, the vast sky above, and no civilization for miles. She'd parked her van on the side of a dirt road—the closest she could get the vehicle after what felt like infinite back roads.

She was far enough away from her vehicle that she intended to camp here for the night. Get the lay of the land and figure out who the keeper of this arrow—too new, too cared for—could be.

She crouched to run a hand over the concrete surface. A slight grain of resistance, but not even a stray blade of grass marred the arrow's appearance.

There was a sense of unease heavy on her shoulders as she set up her tent. Like the beast she'd been chasing all this time had watched her approach and waited until she'd drawn close before morphing. What she thought she knew now felt immensely unknowable.

Wind pressed against the nylon of the tent, making a flapping sound. Ellen yearned for her laptop, for phone service, for the comfort of her readership and their support for her truths. Watching the trees sway in the woods, she even thought fondly of the bored young woman who'd made her coffee back in Reno. Civilians and all their flaws, even the government and its iron fist, were still familiar—still responded to the weight of gravity and the pull of time.

Unlike this arrow. The man from Nevada had said that the markers were one hundred years old, but this one appeared brand new.

Perched on a foldable camping stool, Ellen rested her boot against the very tip of the arrow point. She'd used her compass to determine its angle from end to end, exactly west. Pointing back the way she'd traveled, all these miles. Contrary to every marker she'd passed thus far.

She should've looked ahead. Mapped out the next arrow to know if this one was a fluke. Cursing to herself, she scooped up a fistful of dirt to fling across the yellow paint. Crumbs across a table, marring its perfection.

Ellen pulled out her notebook as night closed in around her crackling campfire. *It's quiet out here, but a quiet that feels like bated breath. Waiting to see if I'll take the next step.*

Before zipping herself inside the tent, she took a single piece of wood from the fire, now doused, and marched to the center of the arrow. She thrust one end of the stick, sooty from the flame, to the flat surface and scraped out three words: *Here I am.*

In the morning, there was a reply. Written beneath Ellen's message in a near unintelligible scrawl:

We know.

ELLEN WASN'T AN idiot.

She wouldn't be lured into a fool's errand. The tempting next step was to Rambo her way across the land in the direction the arrow pointed, but Ellen paused.

A hike back to her van and a drive into the closest town would take hours. Then she'd have to refuel, purchase supplies, make another pass-through of satellite imagery, poke around the county website for parcel maps, update her readers. She was so close to the answers she'd been seeking that her hands shook, and she clenched them into fists.

Disassembling the tent took minutes, organizing her backpack, less time than that. Ellen raised her camera to snap a few more shots; the cloud cover provided good lighting. *Click* went the shutter. She circled around, her back to the open hills, the arrow pointing directly toward the woods. *Click.*

She lifted the lens higher, framing the trees themselves, a football-field length away—*click*—and froze.

A man stood at the very edge of the woods.

Ellen lowered her camera and casually hovered a hand over the holstered Glock on her hip. She couldn't see the man's expression from where she stood, couldn't tell if he feigned friendliness or not. He wore loose clothing, an earthy ochre in color. A ruse, she immediately assumed. Agents of the government wouldn't appear in suits and sunglasses; they'd try to blend in.

As she watched, he lifted an arm and pointed at her.

No, not at her—at the arrow. Ellen glanced down, then back up, gesturing toward the message that had been scrawled sometime in the night. *From you?*

The man nodded. He turned slightly, like he meant to head into the trees, but continued watching her. A clear invitation to follow him.

Ellen considered him. Her body remained tense, panic urging her to flee, to be wary of what was happening. But she'd always prided herself to think deeper than the average Joe, and she worked to keep her wits about her now.

This moment was what she'd been waiting for. A search for an answer, and here was the hinge. Would she proceed or step back? Would she cut short the journey she told her readers she was so determined to see through?

She removed her gun from its holster, exaggerating her movements, letting the man see. She pulled the slide back, racking a round into the chamber, then let the gun hang by her side, aimed at the ground. She checked her GPS, ensuring the coordinates were saved, and took a step toward the woods.

The man waited. As Ellen moved closer, his features became

clearer, and she realized he was smiling. Not a fixed grin, but one that widened the closer she came. Until, when she was ten feet away, she could see all his teeth.

She didn't speak right away. Only stood with her gun, watching him, showing him that she was not afraid. His feet were bare.

"What are the arrows for?" she finally asked. "Where do they lead?"

His smile, impossibly, grew even wider. He spoke: *"Ad maiora."*

Then he turned his back to her and began to run.

HE FLEW ACROSS the ground, under limbs, and between trunks. The man was fast. It was clear he knew these woods. Ellen followed.

His words didn't mean anything to her. A code? A message? Was she supposed to reply with a passphrase?

She considered disabling him, a shot to the leg, but there was no clear danger—no obvious reason why he was sprinting. More than the man, she chased her answer.

She controlled her breathing, short bursts. She'd stayed in shape for moments of action like this. Flashes of yellow appeared on her left and right as she wove between trees. At first, they were too sporadic to comprehend, but as Ellen trailed the man deeper, they appeared more frequently.

More arrows. Bright yellow. Reproductions of the one she'd slept next to the previous night but painted on trunks.

Ellen stumbled but did not fall. Her heart raced, and not just because of the physical exertion. Her backpack thumped against her as she ran, and she thought of her loyal readers who followed her with faith that she would give them answers. She was so close. Too close for this to go unnoticed by the world.

More arrows. More and more and more. There wasn't a tree she passed that didn't have yellow painted on its trunk.

The man was out of sight by now, but Ellen didn't need him; she'd been following arrows for months. Her quest was nearing its end.

Ahead of her, something began to take shape through the trees. Her mind began to thrum: *danger danger danger*. Still Ellen ran, shouting over the warning in her head, drowning it out: "You can't keep your secrets any longer! Here I am!"

Until she saw something that made her stop, hands on her knees as she panted and tried to understand.

Before her was another arrow. A giant arrow, larger than any she'd seen by at least three times.

Somehow, Ellen knew, it was the last arrow.

Danger! her mind repeated.

It was just as pristine as the one she'd camped by. This one was paved between trees, concealed by the canopy.

"Tell me what this means!" Ellen shouted to no one—anyone. "The arrows! What is their purpose?"

There was movement from her left, and she turned, raising the Glock. The man again, this time wearing a pure white sheath and standing at the arrow's tip. Among the trees at his back were others, also dressed in white.

Danger! her mind urged.

"Tell me," Ellen demanded. Her grip on the gun was no longer steady. "I've come all this way. I've stood on every single arrow. I am *here*—" she flung her other hand out, indicating the shape "—and I want to know what it means!"

The man's smile was softer now, almost soothing in appearance. "*Ad maiora*," he said. Then, as if purposely mocking her blank expression, her lack of fluency: "Toward something greater."

Danger!—Hands landed on her. Pulling off her backpack, swatting away her gun, and binding her with rope. She twisted and elbowed, unable to reach the blade in her pocket. She bit someone, hard, and was subsequently gagged. Ellen's brain stopped forming coherent thoughts, leaving only static in her head. She couldn't move for fear of the answer to come, because she knew now, with startling clarity, that the arrows did not lead to a revelation that she would be able to share.

She was dragged across the dirt, toward the man, to the point of the arrow.

He wasn't smiling anymore by the time she was laid at his feet. He simply crouched down and touched a hand to her forehead. "*In articulo mortis*," he murmured. Then, so softly she could barely hear, came the translation. "At point of death."

And Ellen, through the gag, began to scream.

FOR I NEVER WAS SO SMALL

MARISCA PICHETTE

"THE BOX IS pink. Like, bubblegum pink. And tiny."

The color is off-putting. And it's smaller than I expected, only half the size it had been in my head. Maybe that's a good sign; maybe it'll fulfill its promise to make me half the size I am now.

"Better than it saying YOU ARE FAT, I guess." Carla's voice issues from the Google Home next to the toaster. "Are you gonna open it?"

I stare at the barcode, thin black lines mocking me. Skinny, perfect. I grab a knife from the drawer. "Opening it now."

I slice through pink tape (*pig pink*, I think), and peel the box open. Bubble pillows fill the space between me and the most expensive purchase I've made in the past year. I stab them flat one by one, piercing my way down to the printer in its Styrofoam cradle.

I lift the thing, surprised by its weight. It looks like a single-cup Keurig. "I still can't believe how small it is."

"Must be another sign." Carla laughs. I set the printer on the counter and dig through deflated plastic pillows to find the instructions.

"Does it come with ingredients?" Carla asks.

"No, I think it's all inside, pre-loaded."

I scan the instructions, printed on pink paper thin between my fingers. "Step one: connect Print Perfect to power." I remove the plastic cover from the cord and connect it to the outlet. Pink light fills the little chamber where all my meals will be made.

"It glows pink."

Carla snorts. "Do they make it blue for the guys, you think?"

"I don't think they make one for men." The marketing for Print Perfect is painfully gendered. The newest diet sensation: 3D printed food that's filling and tasty, without the dubious additives of Weight Watchers. Part of the fun is supposed to be watching your food being laid down, layer by layer.

I've tried other diets. And yeah, I've also tried "loving myself" and "accepting my body the way it is." That's not as simple as everyone seems to think.

When I'm not crying, I'm imagining ways to turn myself into something else—or nothing at all. That's why I resorted to Print Perfect. For a dream of looking in the mirror and not wanting to break what I see.

"Step two: Enter current weight."

I find a touchpad on the side of the pink printer. Three digits I know by heart. The light inside intensifies.

"What's it doing now?" Carla asks.

I'm sweating through my shirt. "Just being fucking pink."

"Oh, this is exciting. Do you get to choose your first meal?"

I look at the instructions. "Just salty or sweet." Weird.

"Sweet, definitely," Carla says.

I select the dessert icon on the touchpad. Nothing happens. "It's broken."

"Really?"

"Nothing's happening."

"Are you sure you set it up right?"

I feel my face going as pink as the printer. "I'll call you when something happens, okay?" Without waiting for an answer, I hang up.

"Fuck it." I shove the pink instructions in a drawer. I can feel the tears gathering in my eyes. I force them back and grab the pink box and punctured Styrofoam pillows. I cram the accusatory packaging together, desperate to rid myself of the evidence of this new low point in my life.

The summer heat wraps itself around me the minute I step outside. Humidity fills my lungs and I wish I could shed my clothes, peel the skin from my body just to feel lighter, just to feel less oppressed.

The driveway burns my feet, and I scoot onto the grass, making the trip to the bins as quickly as possible. I cast the pink box to the bottom of the recycling and ball up the plastic with the Styrofoam in the trash. Before I feel eyes on me, I rush back inside, locking the door.

Something smells. A mix of chemicals and burnt sugar. *Shit.*

I run into the kitchen. Print Perfect has stopped glowing. In the little chamber, something lies on the dish. As I approach, a chime sounds, nearly giving me a heart attack. The touchpad flashes.

Request Complete. Enjoy!

It takes me a minute to work up the courage to put my hand inside and pick up my first diet meal. It's about the size of a macaron and smells sort of the same. The whiff of chemicals is thankfully dissipating.

My food is round, with little ridges from the printing process. Layers of sugar, I guess, or a low-calorie equivalent. The color is a little off-putting: more pink, nearly neon.

"Well, here goes four hundred dollars." I close my eyes and take a small bite of the not-macaron.

It flakes when I bite in, each layer collapsing between my teeth. It's certainly sweet. Like frosting.

It reminds me a little of baklava, or Neapolitan coconut. After the first shocking sweetness, the taste isn't bad. I take another bite. Another.

In less than twenty seconds, the food is gone.

I activate the touchpad and try to get the printer to make another. I'm met with a digital countdown.

03:59:36

"Four *hours?*"

I grab a bag of chips from the cupboard and leave Print Perfect in the kitchen, retreating with my snack to the couch.

The first chip tastes like nothing. I suck it into softness, wondering if the sweetness of the printed food fucked my taste buds. The second chip is slightly salty. By the fifth, they taste normal again. I finish the bag.

From the couch I can see the printer, its touchpad shining pink, pink, pink.

I'M NOT HUNGRY, but I stay up until the four-hour lock runs out. I stand at the counter, finger hovering over my two choices: salty or sweet. I find myself craving the macaron again, but curiosity prompts me to select the salty option.

Once again, the pad goes dark, and nothing happens. This time, I stay and wait.

Deep in the printer's pink heart, something hums. In the chamber, something squirts down onto the dish. It smells like chemicals and popcorn. My mouth waters as the next meal is printed, layer by layer.

The chime makes me jump again. I forgot how loud it is. I reach inside and pick up my tiny morsel.

It's about the same size as the sweet meal, but more rounded. Like a dinner roll, I guess. I turn it over in my hands, feeling its artificial ridges.

I didn't think I was hungry, but the not-roll smells good. I take a bite.

It tastes like bacon and Doritos and something else I can't quite grasp. I eat the whole thing in three bites and lick the crumbs from my fingers.

"Okay, you're not a total waste of money." I wipe my hands on my thighs and stretch, feeling truly full now. As I turn to go to bed, I glimpse the countdown on the touchpad.

07:59:42

"*Eight* hours now?"

I step back from the gleaming screen. Does it know I'm about to go to bed? The thing must have an internal clock.

On my way out of the kitchen I pick up the empty chip bag and throw it in the trash.

MY DREAMS ARE pink. I wake up starving.

I brush my teeth and go downstairs. Before booting up my laptop, I go to check on Print Perfect. Still ten minutes left on the timer.

"Real food it is then." I grab a brown banana and force myself to eat half. It tastes like papier-mâché. I throw the rest away.

My stomach is killing me. I brew coffee and stare at the countdown. Finally, it finishes. I pull up the menu. There are two new options for printing.

Hydration (Caffeinated)

Hydration (Decaffeinated)

"What? You can't print drinks. Liquid doesn't layer." I scroll back to the sweet and salty options. I pick up my coffee and take a sip.

It tastes like dishwater. I spit it back into the mug and check the coffee maker. I'm sure I set it up right. Has the coffee gone stale?

My phone rings.

"Hey, Carla."

The Google Home lights up as the Bluetooth connects. "Did you try it? Did you eat something?"

"Yeah, I had some snacks last night. They taste pretty good, actually."

"Do they look like cyborg food?"

"Shut up."

After another awful sip, I pour my coffee down the drain. "I was just about to have it make breakfast."

"Ooh, exciting. What can it make? Can you have low-carb waffles?"

"It only makes small stuff. I just pick salty or sweet."

"Sounds like *Alice in Wonderland.* 'Eat me.' 'Drink me.' Just make sure you get the one that makes you smaller, not bigger." She snorts.

It's easy to ignore her, with my stomach aching for food. I select salty. The touchpad goes dark.

"Did you lose any weight yet?"

"Dude, it's been less than twenty-four hours."

"Come on! They say this thing is like magic. Go check!"

Carla isn't even here, and she's telling me what to do. I look at the printer. It'll take a minute or two to make my breakfast. "Fine. I'll be right back."

I go upstairs and pull the bathroom scale out of my closet. I hide it in a different place every week, as if that helps. Can't hide it from the person doing the hiding. As I step onto it, my bare feet shocked by cold steel, I imagine the number I will see: three digits of constant shame.

I close my eyes. I don't want to open them and see the number hasn't changed.

It never changes. Not for long, at least.

After a few seconds, I hear the distant chime of the printer, then Carla talking. *Shit.* I open my eyes and look down at the scale.

I step off. I step on.

What?

I step off again. Carla's calling my name. I smell chemicals and sausage. I run downstairs.

"Drew? You there?"

"Five pounds!" I yell. "Five fucking pounds!"

"I told you! The thing's magic!" The Google Home flashes with Carla's words. I slide against the counter, breathless.

How did I lose five pounds? I ate two snacks that tasted decidedly unhealthy, plus a bag of chips. And overnight? There's no way.

I look at myself in the window. I don't look thinner. Do I?

"What was that chime?" Carla asks.

I turn from my reflection to the pink glow. "Breakfast."

Print Perfect holds what looks like a patty. I pick it up, ridges revealing its falseness. "I think it made me tofu, or something."

"What's it taste like?"

The first bite is dry and dense. When I swallow, I feel my hunger. I eat the rest of the patty in two bites and lick my fingers clean.

"Tastes amazing," I say, though I barely paid attention. The countdown is back.

05:59:48

"Shit. Six hours."

"Six hours? Six hours till what?"

"'Til I can print something else."

"Oh, what the fuck. That's so long. What are you supposed to do in the meantime?"

I look up at my cabinets. I know what I have in the house: low-carb snacks and rotting produce. None of it appeals.

"I'm going out. My coffee was shit. Talk later?"

"Sure thing. Bye, Drew."

"Bye, Carla."

The Google Home falls silent. I grab my keys and brave the heat outside.

"SERIOUSLY?" MY ICED coffee tastes like water. I look at the label: three sugars added. Yeah, right.

I pour it out onto the grass and climb back into my stifling car. *What a waste of money.*

By the time I get home again, there are ten emails waiting in my inbox, mostly follow-up questions to my last freelance assignment. I decide to work out my drink later and just have tap water for now. Sitting down to work, I take a lukewarm sip. It's even more unsatisfying than usual.

When I next look at the clock, it's 5:38 p.m. *Did I really just go through the whole day without a snack?* I should be starving.

But I'm not.

I close my laptop and run upstairs. Part of me is afraid the five pounds I lost will be back, water weight gained from a single glass over nine hours.

I close my eyes when I step onto the scale. After a few breaths, I open them.

Five pounds. Five *more* pounds.

I've lost ten pounds since yesterday.

I throw the scale into my closet and run downstairs. Print Perfect is waiting, touchpad glowing pink.

I conjure my options. I'm tempted to select sweet as a reward, but I've barely had anything to drink all day.

Against my better judgment, I select *Hydration (Caffeinated)*.

The screen goes dark. I hear the hum inside and watch the printer pour layers of something not-liquid. When the chime sounds, a sphere rests on the dish.

It's squishy to the touch, like Jell-o. I give it a cautious sniff; the off-brown color isn't appealing. It smells like Red Bull and cocoa. I lick it.

Drink me. I bite in.

Everything sharpens. When I take a second bite, the printer seems to glow all over. Colors are brighter, shapes more clearly defined.

"Wow." I swallow the last of the sphere. Better than any energy drink I've had before.

I open my laptop again. I work halfway into the night before I remember I never ate dinner, let alone lunch. When I go back to the printer at 2 o'clock, the countdown shines in the dark.

04:24:16

I can't have anything until the morning. I should sleep off the—but no, there's no hunger.

I should still sleep, I think as I go back to my laptop and sit down. *I'll just finish a few things first. I'll sleep soon.*

When exhaustion hits me at last, it's light outside. I look at the clock.

"Oh my god."

It's 7:30 already. I'd be getting up in half an hour. Shit.

Getting to my feet feels wrong, like my body's bent out of shape. I look down at myself. My baggy clothes. My bare feet. My...

Nausea turns my stomach. I need to eat something. I need coffee.

I stumble into the kitchen. The printer glows like the dawn.

What do I pick? Caffeine or food? How long will I have to wait for the other once my choice has been made?

"I should buy another of these," I say to myself, swaying against the counter. I could alternate between them, never having to wait. But I can't drop another four hundred dollars right now. Rent is due soon.

The fogginess wins out. I select hydration again. That's the most important thing, isn't it? I close my eyes and rest my forehead on the printer until the chime jerks me back. This sphere is darker than the last one. I hope that means there's more caffeine.

I eat it in four bites, gelatin dissolving on my tongue.

Immediately, I feel better. I sigh, my hunger dribbling away. *So, hydration helps with hunger, too.* I look at my reflection in the window. The relief fades.

I don't look a pound lighter.

Upstairs, I drag the scale out of the closet. I've lost almost twenty pounds since the printer arrived. Staring at my feet on the scale, I realize they look thinner. My stomach—how didn't I notice when I saw my reflection in the window? It's flatter. Even my boobs seem smaller.

I step off the scale and go into the bathroom. *When did I last need to pee?* I must be really dehydrated. I pull down yesterday's pants and sit on the toilet. Nothing comes.

After a minute of waiting, I stand up and look at myself in the mirror. It's…

I turn to the side, look down, really *scrutinize* myself. I look up at the mirror.

They don't…

They don't match.

In the mirror, I'm just as fat as before. In real life, I'm losing weight. Losing it faster than I ever have.

"The scale's right," I say aloud. "The mirror's wrong."

I go downstairs and open my computer. Behind me, Print Perfect counts down.

11:56:05

CARLA CALLS THAT night. "How's it going?"

"Twenty pounds down," I tell her, leaning on the counter. I've got four minutes left until I can print something new. I haven't had anything since this morning.

"Damn, girl. You're on fire. I should really think about getting one of those. But I'd end up cheating all the time."

"There's no point," I say, watching the timer. "I'm not hungry. Not until, like, right before the printer's countdown finishes. Or if I miss it. Then I'm starving."

"How Pavlovian." She chuckles, then gasps. "Oh! This weekend let's go shopping! We can pick out new clothes for you."

I look down at myself. My clothes are way too big now. "Yeah, good idea." I think about all the styles I'll be able to wear—once I lose a few more pounds. I'm almost Carla's size now; I can't wait for her to see.

"How long are you going to stick to the diet?" Carla asks. "A month?"

I hadn't thought about that. "I spent four hundred dollars on this thing. Shouldn't I use it as long as possible? Until the ingredients run out or something?"

Thirty seconds left on the countdown. I can't take my eyes off it.

"Might be unhealthy. Additives and whatever else they put in. Besides, I'm sure you miss real food." I can hear the shrug in Carla's voice.

Time's up.

"This is real food," I say, selecting salty. The printer's hum makes my mouth water. *Eat me.*

"Drew, it might be *made* with real food, but I've seen the ads. That stuff does *not* look like food. It looks like doll food."

"Sounds like you're just mad it's not Insta-worthy." At the chime, I pull out my single cube that smells of toast and cheese and beer. I take a bite. *Perfect.*

"I gotta get some more work done. I'll talk to you tomorrow."

"Drew? It's like 8:30 p.m."

I hang up on her and eat my food.

AFTER A WEEK, I'm half the weight I was. Carla wants to go shopping, but I don't want to go too far from Print Perfect. I tell her I'm not thin enough yet. I tell her I'll call her back.

I now have to wait twenty hours between drinks, thirty between meals. I work on my laptop while I wait, but I don't really register what I do throughout the day. I know I respond to emails and shop online, but I don't remember what I see or say. When I lie down, I count my ribs. They remind me of layers of nutrients, printed in pink light.

None of my clothes fit now. It's so hot that I stop wearing them, walking around naked so I can always see how far I've come. I count my knuckles and the bones in my feet. I feel the spaces in between my arm bones and the nubs of my vertebrae.

I used to be soft and squishy. Now I'm hard, uneven. I love it.

But it's not enough. Not yet. I'm not hungry until the timer finishes, and then nothing will sate me except one of the four options on the little pink touchpad. I move my laptop into the kitchen so I can always see it. I spend hours watching the numbers tick down.

I haven't been upstairs in days. I bring the scale down to the kitchen.

Carla keeps calling. I send her to voicemail half the time.

Today, I have the decaf drink. It's the shape of an egg and smells like celery. I swallow it whole and watch the screen give me forty hours until my next meal.

I sleep with my head pressed to the cold metal of the scale.

I'VE DRAWN ALL the curtains and covered the mirrors. They're broken. They don't show me how I really am.

I've lost over a hundred pounds. The scale barely registers my weight. But the mirrors say I'm fat. The windows use darkness to maintain the lie.

I know what I am. I can count my ribs and the tendons in my jaw. I can see my veins and fold myself as flat as my laptop.

The only thing that doesn't lose weight is my head. It's now the biggest thing about me. I see it in the reflection of my computer screen. I feel its weight when I lie down.

I need to know how to make it thin, too. I need to know how to make it match the rest of me.

SIXTY HOURS UNTIL my next meal. Carla left me a voicemail. I delete it without listening.

I think I know how to fix my body.

I climb the stairs on all fours and find my razor. I haven't been to the bathroom in weeks. There's been no need.

Squatting on the tile floor, I shave my head. I leave the hair where it falls.

I don't know whether it's day or night. I go back downstairs and wait by Print Perfect.

I'M SO HUNGRY. But Print Perfect won't work.

I've plugged it in and unplugged it, pressed all the buttons. I even dug out the pink instructions and searched for an explanation, to no avail.

I looked in the cupboards. There's nothing but expired food that tastes like ash and gets caught in my throat. Lying on the floor, I call Carla.

"Help."

"Drew?"

"It broke. I can't… I can't eat."

"Drew, where are you?"

"In the kitchen."

"Drink some water, okay? I'll come over."

Water? I stare at my phone. *What's water?*

Hydration. She means hydration. But the printer's broken. I try to remember where else to get hydration. Next to Print Perfect: something like a bird, like a bath. I haul myself up the side of the counter and into the farmhouse sink, drawing my legs to my chest. I didn't realize I could fit.

My back wedged against stainless steel, I start crying, shaking and shaking, but no tears will come. Nothing leaves my weightless eyes. Nothing gives form to my pain.

"How's it work?" I ask the air, gasping my words. I stare at the faucet, curved like a perfect swan's neck. I see the taps on either side, squat and inelegant. *Tweedledum and Tweedledee.*

I drag my arm across my body, reaching for them. The task feels impossible, but finally I'm able to grasp one. I pull with all my diminished weight.

The water comes out faster than I remember. It hits me with a vengeance, tearing my flesh open—my delicate skin now thin as paper.

I scream. Water and blood and water fill the sink, fill me. It's not right it's not it's not right. I try to switch it off but I'm not strong enough. I'm wedged in the sink, turning into gelatin. I can't get out. I can't escape.

Struggling to escape, fingers slipping on the smooth edges of my steel casket, trying to hold myself closed, I scream and sob into the empty house. But the doors are locked and the curtains drawn, and I'm too light to flee the current washing me around and around, pulling my flesh into the drain.

Will I fit? I bleed and swirl and bleed. Surely, I'm not that small.

But as my head lolls and I stare down at the horrible hole, I fear I will.

Every part of me will drain away, nothing left to clog the pipes and save me from drowning.

Carla—where's Carla? *She's late, late. Too late to save me.*

As red water creeps up to my chin, my tears run down at last to meet it. Saline and blood, rising, rising. And with it comes the tail end of a broken fairy tale.

Opening my mouth to scream, I can only drink.

I wish I hadn't cried so much.

My blood tastes salty and sweet.

PRODIGAL

CHRIS McGRANE

I WANT YOU to know that I forgive you.

You couldn't know what that community would do to you.

They are specialists at warping young minds.

Turning them against their friends, turning them against their families.

I've seen it happen before.

I tried to warn you, but you were young and impulsive.

You had just turned 18 and were eager to spread your wings.

You didn't need me anymore, or so you told me.

You rejected the beautiful home your mother and I had made for you.

When you left to "find your own place in the world," I didn't know whether to cry or to burst with pride.

You were always my favorite child, and I indulged you.

I gave you your freedom.

I let them poison your mind.

I let them steal you from me.

I should have seen the warning signs.

I should never have trusted them.

But I trusted you. When you told me that they were your friends and were treating you well, making you happy, I believed you.

I believed you, until the day you wrote me a letter, accusing me of hideous crimes, telling me you never wanted to see me or the rest of your family again.

I blame myself.

I let them turn you into a Trojan horse that would destroy everything I held dear, as surely as they destroyed Hector's house. They weren't satisfied with stealing only one of my children.

Once they had you, they wouldn't stop until they had taken the others.

They are not your family. They destroy families with their lies. They brainwash young minds. I know that you never would have betrayed me, denounced me, otherwise. The cruel language you used against me, it sounded nothing like you. I knew those words had been placed in your mouth.

It wasn't your fault.

That is why today, I write you this letter to invite you back home with open arms.

I am still your father. We are still your family, and we forgive you. You belong to me and always will.

We love you, despite the pain.

When you spoke against me, they acted.

They sent the police and the FBI and the others to my home.

They had wanted to destroy me for decades, but now they had "proof".

Now they had a "witness" who would repeat their lies in a court of law.

We learned of their plans to raid our house and destroy our family. However, with God's assistance, we escaped, as Moses escaped the pharaoh.

I am relieved that they did not force you to return to your biological family–the family you fled at the age of 14.

I cannot imagine what a torment it would have been for you. Then again, I cannot imagine why you would want to return to the outside world, knowing what a hell it had been for you.

It has now been almost four years since the FBI raid.

I have searched for you ever since, my child. I have searched for you constantly.

Any father would do the same.

I rejoice to have found you again.

You may scream in fear as I approach you, but I will not recoil. I know the lies they have told you about me.

Don't be afraid, child. I am not angry. My heart is filled with love for you. I would slaughter the fatted calf to celebrate your return.

I am still your father. You belong to me and always will.

It hurts my heart that you kept the news of your pregnancy from me. How could you possibly believe I would harm the baby? Or you?

Did your psychologists, those professional deceivers, poison your mind so thoroughly, that you forgot all the wonderful times we spent together?

You now leave your child in the care of strangers while you spend time studying how to indoctrinate young minds with the psychologists' lies. Every moment you are not studying this insane propaganda, you are working for mammon's cause.

I have never harmed a child. Can you really say the same? Every day, you leave him in the company of strangers, for hours at a time. They are not his family. These strangers do not love him. They love only the money you pay them.

I cannot bear to see such a beautiful child raised in such a poisonous environment.

You must understand that that is why I rescued him.

Your voice on the phone is so full of rage, so full of hate, that it shocks me.

Once again, you are the tool of the liars. A puppet of the psychologists, and the FBI and all those others who seek to destroy my family and my ministry.

I rescued you. I gave you a home when the world would not. I gave you a place in my family when your own rejected you.

I gave you the purpose that you so desperately craved. I gave you the love that the world denied you.

I gave you light, when your days were filled with darkness.

I gave you hope, when the world had convinced you to despair.

I gave you food, when you had none.

I washed away your sins with my pain and with my blood.

And how do you repay me?

You repay each kindness with an evil lie. You scheme to destroy me, the man who saved you. You send strangers to take my children. You send armed men to persecute my disciples. You send Caesar's soldiers to crucify me.

Yet still, I forgive you.

The FBI are cunning as snakes. They fool my sentries.

They storm my home. Do not believe their lies. I did not start this war. I did not booby-trap my own home. I did not choose to make martyrs of my family. The psychologists and police did that.

I am so relieved my followers found you in time.

You are the prodigal one and I rejoice that you are returned to me.

Don't try to talk. Do not struggle. I have given you and your child something to help you relax.

Sleep now, my dear children. When you awake, it will be in my Father's house.

I will be there to welcome you, because you both belong to me.

You always will.

UNDERFOOT

KALEIGH RODGERSON

THE PROBLEM WITH most grown-ups, Lessa figures, is that they always have pinched feet.

This is why she always goes barefoot, like a sensible person. Muffled shouts echo from the next room over, as if proving the point.

Hanging off the couch, her hair and arms framed against the floor, she ignores the shouting until Mom walks into the sitting room and looks at her. "Get your feet off the wall."

Lessa wriggles her toes.

Mom calls over her shoulder, "At least our daughter has the excuse of being a child, John—you don't!"

Dad responds with muffled swearing. Lessa eyes her mother's high heels and clenches her toes in sympathy. She'd be angry, too, if she had to walk in those.

"Now you're making excuses for bad parenting," Dad shouts back. His thin frame enters the sitting room. He's wearing brown sneakers. "You always put the blame on someone else!"

"Excuse me," Mom snaps. "Was it my fault when you went to a bar with my *cousin* on our *anniversary*—"

Lessa's older sister Ivy stomps into the room, looks around, and drops her shiny bag by the couch. Her shoes are gray, proper, and pointy. Mom always says it's important to look respectable, but Lessa has noticed that the clothes they wear outside are much nicer than the house's interior, with its battered furniture and stained rugs.

Ivy yanks Lessa upright on the couch. She stumbles,

complaining, "No, Ivy! I wanted all the blood to go to my head! So it would pop!"

"God, you're crazy too," Ivy mutters. Ivy says lots of weird things like that and never explains. It doesn't matter though, because she adds, "Put on your shoes—I'm taking you to the carnival."

IT'S ONLY WHEN they get outside that Lessa remembers her sister can't drive. She reaches up, tugging at Ivy's hand. "Hey! Hey, are we walking?" she demands, looking down at her feet. She hates all shoes, but she especially hates the glossy ones Ivy just forced on her. Shiny hard shoes, a pink skirt, white shirt. Mother will *scream* if Lessa comes back dirty. And she probably will. She doesn't want to walk in these.

"It's too far to walk, dummy," says Ivy. An unfamiliar car rolls into the driveway.

Lessa doesn't know anything about cars, but this one has a lot of odd angles. It's shiny, too, which she assumes means expensive. Then she sees the driver. "Oh—it's Colin. I thought you weren't talking to him anymore?"

"So did I," sighs Ivy. But she tugs Lessa's hand toward the car.

Colin gets out and stoops to kiss Ivy on the cheek. He pats Lessa's head, but he does it so hard she squeaks a protest. He's nearly as old as their dad. "Both of my girls! Ready to have some fun?"

"Yeah!" says Lessa.

Ivy doesn't say anything. She hesitates after Colin gets in the car, then slides into the back with Lessa, still holding her hand. Colin shoots them an annoyed look but doesn't comment.

Lessa takes her shoes off. Ivy rolls her eyes. "You can't walk outside like that," she says as they pull up to the carnival. Bright, flashing lights color the interior of the car. Muffled but cheerful music reaches them; in the distance, Lessa can see the top of a Ferris wheel.

"Just act normal for once, okay?" Ivy mutters.

Privately, Lessa thinks Ivy would be a lot happier if she weren't wearing heels and a tight dress and a lipstick-smile. But she smells fried dough and peanuts in the air, so she puts the shoes on again.

Colin has a lot of money. Lessa knows this because her parents talk about it all the time. He pays for the tickets, then an elephant ear for Lessa when she points them out. Ivy intervenes when he tries to get her cotton candy, too, and says maybe later.

Colin also pays for the games they play. Lessa tosses about a hundred balls at some cups, but never knocks them down, so he buys her a little stuffed horse. He nudges Ivy into trying a dart game. She sighs but obliges him and tosses the little darts at yellow and blue balloons. The carnival worker leans over his table.

"You should be careful with that one," he says to Colin, nodding toward Lessa while she examines the prizes. "I've never seen a carnival here so empty. On account of all the missing kids, you know."

"Oh, she'll be fine," says Colin. Ivy misses the next throw and bites her lip, staring at the ground.

"I'm just saying," the stranger insists. "Keep her close."

"Oh, we will," says Colin. He drapes an arm around Ivy, tugging her to his side. "This one, too! My girlfriend's great with kids, you know." He winks.

Ivy takes Lessa's hand again when they walk away.

After the Ferris wheel, Colin buys them sticks of fluffy cotton candy. Then they go on a swirling teacup ride, which is a mistake, because Lessa steps off the platform and immediately vomits.

That ends the night pretty fast.

"I REALLY DON'T think we have the money for it," Mom says.

Lessa scribbles on her coloring book, only half-listening. She's working on a picture of a cat hiding under a bench. It's surrounded by butterflies and flowers, which she's already covered in bright fluorescent shades. She's heard this talk about money—or the lack of it—before. She wishes she had a cat, but Mom said they're expensive and gross and unclean.

"We've got the money, we'll get the money," says Dad. "We'll have it soon, I mean."

"We don't have the money until it's *official.* She's only sixteen. He could change his mind, even after… It's not like we can make a contract. I'm just saying that we should wait."

"What, do you think he's lying? He's no liar. Everything's going to be fine." Dad steps closer. Bends down beside Lessa. "That's nice, Lessa. But don't you think the cat's a little mean-looking?"

"Nuh-uh," says Lessa. "My teacher said cats eat their kittens, sometimes. This one's a bad mom and ate them *all.*"

After a moment reflecting on this, Lessa grabs up a red crayon. In broad strokes, she draws blood gushing from the cat's mouth.

"…Uh, creative," says Dad. Mom declares she's going outside to "clear her head" and smoke. She does both these things a lot.

LESSA USED TO walk home alone from school, but she can't do that anymore. The school made all sorts of new rules because some kids in the lower grades disappeared. She isn't even supposed to walk to the park now!

Ivy still gets to leave home alone, or with Colin. She's usually with Colin, even though she doesn't look happy about it and said they were breaking up.

Lessa isn't supposed to talk about Colin to anyone. Dad says his relationship with Ivy is "romantic" but that people "wouldn't understand," which Lessa supposes is a good thing, because the best love stories are always kind of sad and no one wants the couple to be together. Last year, Lessa dated this kid in her class, Michael Foster, for two days. Then he pinched her arm so hard she cried, so she threw dirt in his face, and the teacher made *her* miss recess the next day even though Michael totally started it. At least Colin doesn't do stuff like that with Ivy.

And he's always nice to Lessa. He likes kids a lot; says he wants his own someday. Ivy doesn't, but Mom says that's silly, and she'll change her mind soon. She always adds, "You need to make Colin happy, dear."

Lessa would usually pester Ivy into walking with her to the park. But it's raining outside, and Mom will yell really loud if she tracks mud back. So, she goes into Ivy's room and climbs into her bed, plopping herself against Ivy's side.

Ivy sighs, like this is some big bother. But she's not even doing anything—just sitting, staring at the wall, and listening to sad wailing music. The singer keeps warbling their voice like they're going to cry. But it's better than Dad's country songs, Lessa supposes. "Hey. Hey." Lessa pokes her toe into her sister's thigh. Ivy doesn't look at her. "Come *on*. You're so boring."

Ivy snorts. "I wish!"

"You are so," Lessa says. "Play a game with me."

"No."

"Please?" Lessa asks. Mom always says she needs to use her manners, but it never helps, because Ivy just refuses again.

So Lessa persists, and when Ivy tries to leave, she grabs onto her sister's leg and lets Ivy drag her across the floor. Ivy keeps walking, pausing by the fridge to try shaking her off. It doesn't work.

"I said please!" Lessa whines.

"Ugh, fine." Ivy relents.

Lessa cheers and runs to find a game.

They play *Chutes and Ladders*. Ivy wins every time. "That was too easy," Ivy says.

"That's not nice!" Lessa isn't that bad at the game, is she? "Let's play another."

Ivy shakes her head. "I think I'm done."

"Aw, come on. You're no fun. Mom and Dad never want to play either."

Ivy frowns. "Don't they?"

"Dad just watches TV." And Lessa doesn't know what Mom does, exactly, but sometimes when she goes out to smoke, she'll be gone for hours.

Ivy sits awhile. She gets like this sometimes, quiet with her own thoughts. Lessa doesn't understand how anyone can be that quiet. She taps her leg impatiently.

Finally, Ivy asks, "Are you happy, Lessa?" She pauses, then adds, "Like, with our family?"

"Yeah?" Lessa considers. "Ice cream would make me *really* happy."

"Too easy," Ivy repeats. She gets up and fetches them both some ice cream. While Lessa eats, Ivy braids her hair. "You've got really nice hair," she says, soft. "And you're going to be so pretty… I wish you weren't."

Lessa pats her cheek. Her hand leaves behind sticky chocolate; oops. "You're pretty, too," she assures her sister.

"I know," says Ivy. "I love you, Lessa." Then she wipes Lessa's fingers and puts away the game board.

IVY DOESN'T GO to school the next day.

Mom seems annoyed, but Lessa doesn't think much about it until she gets back from school and Ivy isn't at home. Her dad comes home from work, talks to Mom in hushed tones, and takes the car out again.

Then Colin comes over to the house, but Mom just steps outside and talks to him for a minute, so Lessa only sees him out the window and he doesn't even say hello. When Mom gets back inside, Lessa asks, "Is Ivy spending the night with him?"

"Of course not," says Mom. But she won't say where Ivy is.

The next day after school, there's a cop outside Lessa's house.

The cop's a woman, and she's really friendly. She comes inside and sits with Lessa on the couch while her parents wait in the kitchen, which seems a little odd. She asks when Lessa last saw Ivy, and if she ever talked about going anywhere or had any dangerous friends.

Lessa tells her she last saw Ivy before going to bed, and she doesn't have any friends, really. Colin doesn't count as a "friend," and he's always nice, not scary. Plus, Lessa isn't supposed to talk about Colin. Her dad said so.

The cop stays a bit. She goes into Ivy's room for a long time, and she takes a bag with some of Ivy's photos and notebooks with her when she leaves. Lessa asks Mom if Ivy will be back for dinner.

Her mom says, "Probably not."

COLIN KEEPS VISITING, even though Lessa isn't there.

That's not *too* strange. But Lessa kind of forgot that he knew Dad before he dated Ivy. They used to work together, except Colin's father owned a really big company and now Colin does, too. Colin used to be married, but his wife died. Dad was the one who suggested he should date Ivy.

Colin doesn't seem happy. He's still nice when he sees Lessa, but when he looks away his smiles always vanish. Mom sends Lessa to her room, and she can hear them talking, then shouting. It's difficult to make out much of the conversation.

"…sixteen…promise…told you we shouldn't…why'd she need to graduate, anyway…"

"…payment…just a bit…won't be long…where could she even…"

Lessa gets bored after a while. She rifles around and finds some old make-up Ivy gave her. She braids her hair and puts on some lipstick, red and sticky. It's a mistake. She looks at herself in a mirror and she's not pretty, like Ivy always was. She looks a bit like the clowns she saw at the carnival. She huffs and goes to wash it off.

Colin sees her when she steps out into the hallway. "Hey, Lessa," he says. He steps in front of her, swinging her up onto his hip. He studies her for a minute. Smiles. "Do you miss Ivy?"

Lessa shrugs.

Colin turns to her dad, cuddling Lessa close. She looks down. Colin has reddish-brown mud all over his expensive boots. She wonders why. Doesn't he work in an office? Colin tells her dad, "I've got an idea."

SO, THEY SAY that in a few years *Lessa* is going to marry Colin, not Ivy.

Lessa's a little excited, because wedding dresses are really pretty and the parties have tons of flowers. But won't Ivy be sad?

Colin assures her that Ivy won't mind.

THINGS ARE A lot less fun without Ivy, but Colin still comes by to take her places. They go to the park a lot, and sometimes they go for really long walks. If Colin sees a kid alone, he always insists Lessa talk to them. He asks lots of questions about where they live and their parents' schedules, and sometimes he offers to drive them places.

So it's not like Lessa's lonely. But Mom and Dad seem even more unhappy than before. Their arguments get louder. Sometimes Lessa can go days without saying more than a few words to them. Dad keeps pacing, even though his shoes get full of holes and he doesn't replace them.

Mom stops reviewing Lessa's homework. "You're a big girl," she tells Lessa. "And this isn't important, anyway."

Lessa spends a lot of time in Ivy's room. Ivy's music is still ugly, but Lessa kind of likes it anyway. When the singers sound sad it's almost like someone is crying with her.

IVY COMES HOME at the start of June, without any warning.

Lessa is playing jump rope in their yard. When she sees her sister she screeches, stumbles over the rope, and skins her knee. She ignores it and launches herself at her alarmed sister. "IvyIvyIvy!"

Mom and Dad come outside. They don't seem as happy, but Mom gives them a tight-lipped smile and says, "I'm glad you're okay, honey." Ivy doesn't smile back.

Mom and Dad want to talk to Ivy alone, which is completely unfair when she *just* got back. Ivy squeezes Lessa's shoulder. "It's okay. I'm not going to leave you again, promise. Why don't you go pick out a game? We'll play it later."

So Lessa does. She finally decides on *Battleship*. It's not Lessa's favorite, but Ivy likes it. She hears shouting, again, coming from the kitchen. Something about Ivy being selfish. A door slams.

Ivy comes into the room and hugs her. "Colin's coming over tomorrow," she says dully.

"Oh." Lessa thinks about this. "Are you sad because I'm going to marry him?"

Ivy draws back, staring. "What?"

"Because he can only marry one person," Lessa explains.

"…No. No, I'm not sad because of that." Ivy pets her hair, silent for a minute. "Let's play the game, okay? And…we might play something else, later."

Lessa doesn't understand what she means by that until after she goes to bed. She sleeps fine, but rouses in complete darkness with someone shaking and shaking her. She sits up, and eventually her eyes adjust enough to see Ivy's outline.

"We're going outside," Ivy whispers. "It's a game. A secret, okay? So be really quiet." She tugs Lessa outside, and for once doesn't chide her to look for shoes.

This turns out to be kind of inconvenient, Lessa discovers, when she almost immediately steps on a thistle. She tries to head back inside for a bandage, but Ivy just scoops her up. "It's okay—I'll carry you. We won't be walking far."

They creep past eight houses to the end of the street. Ivy ducks against a tree there, hidden from the road. "What game are we playing?" Lessa asks.

"We're hiding," says Ivy. "From Mom and Dad."

"Oh. Were you playing a game before, too? Is that why you were gone? I don't think they know we're playing."

"They know," says Ivy. "But we're going to win."

A car rolls by—and then it stops, right on the side of the road, instead of continuing. The door opens. "Come on," Ivy tells her. "This is my friend."

Ivy's friend is a young woman with a shock of pink, curly hair and three tattoos on her bare arms. Ivy sets Lessa on her lap, but Lessa leans over, staring. "Woah," she says. "I want pink hair, Ivy!"

The woman laughs. "Maybe one day, kid," she says. Her voice is hoarse and gravelly, like Dad's after he smokes. She looks a few years older than Ivy. "I'm glad you got her in time. We're about ready to get moving. Totally off the grid, don't worry."

"Right," says Ivy, and starts petting Lessa's hair again.

IT TAKES ALMOST two hours to reach their destination. Lessa only knows this because when she blinks awake, the time on the dashboard is different. Then she sees orange-peach streaks coming over the horizon. "I'm going to miss school," she tells Ivy.

"That's okay," Ivy says. "You're going to get a new teacher."

The car stops. Lessa steps out and her foot promptly reminds her about the thistle. So Ivy carries her over to a group of people.

"Oh, I'm so glad you're all right!" a man cries. He hugs Ivy, incidentally squishing Lessa against her chest. He smells musty and smoky and just plain bad. "You did it! We were all so worried for you, Lessa."

"Um, okay," says Lessa. She's a bit hungry, and wonders if all these people are going to get breakfast or something.

"Sorry—I'm Tomas," he says. "Tom, for you. And this is my family! *You're* my family, now."

"Oh," says Lessa. "Are you my cousin?"

Tom laughs like she told a joke. Some of the other girls do, too. "Labels don't matter. We're family," he repeats. "And families help each other! Like I'm helping you and Ivy here. You're going to come live with us now."

"…But what about Mom and Dad?" Lessa asks, twisting to look at Ivy. "And Colin?"

Something flickers over Tom's face, gone in an instant. "There are no other men in the family, love. You don't have to worry about him. Everything's going to be better, you'll see. I love your sister very much, do you know that?"

Lessa considers this. Did Colin ever say he loved Ivy? Did Ivy say it back? She doesn't think so.

"We've still got a lot of driving to do," Tom says. "Why don't you get to know the girls, and we'll head out."

Lessa is sleepy and hungry, but everyone wants to hug her and say how glad they are that she's here. Lessa tolerates this as she always tolerated family gatherings before. She clings to Ivy through it all, and when at last people start moving toward the cars again, she leans close to whisper in her sister's ear. "I don't think I like it here," she pleads. "Ivy, can we go home?"

"This is our home now. We'll be happier here."

But Ivy doesn't sound happy. "So you're gonna marry Tom?"

"…Not marry, maybe. But I love him."

"But why do I—"

"You'll be happy. I promise. We'll be together and we won't have to…we'll be happy. And you don't have to wear shoes anymore," Ivy tries, smiling weakly. A lot of the girls don't have them. Two are barely wearing any clothes at all. "Isn't that worth it, Lessa?"

But Lessa doesn't think it is. And she notices that, just like Colin, Tom has red mud on his boots. Ivy holds her close as they get back in the car.

"Who is Colin going to marry now?" she asks; but Ivy pretends not to hear.

RAMBUTAN

JADE JIAO

"I CAN'T DO another English-teaching stint," Anika said. She sat on the side of the pavement and pressed a cold beer can to her forehead, eyes fixed on the hazy orange sky.

"It's not that bad," muttered Millie. She was distracted, texting.

"No," said Anika. "I think I'd go home before dealing with kids again, never mind grown men—it's like a pervert gauntlet." She downed the last of her drink. "I'm starving. Let's go get some idiots to buy us some food."

Millie took one last look at her phone and nodded.

"Who are you texting?" said Anika.

"No one, just replying to my mum." She slipped the phone into her pocket.

Millie knew she was getting on Anika's nerves. She hadn't said anything explicitly, but she'd been snide and impatient with Millie for weeks. Their grim, super-economy lodgings didn't help the situation. Neither did the barely functional air conditioner that sputtered and groaned throughout the night, or the dead cockroaches entombed in the yellowing, plastic ceiling light. They both knew something had to change. Between them, Millie was confident they'd work it out, one way or another.

They'd been in Thailand for almost two months. Money had been fairly tight since the start; but now they were down to the last dregs of their overdrafts. They'd begun their trip in Vietnam before covering Laos and moving down through Chang Rai, picking up illegal, foreigner-friendly jobs until they'd found themselves in Bangkok. It was actually Millie who had been to the city before, two years ago while they were still in the midst of their undergrad degrees. But with Anika's confidence, you wouldn't know it. She remained the leader; to have it any other way would dismantle the whole basis of their relationship. Anika had always been the stronger and more confident of the two, prettier and more popular, *the bulldozer.*

The city thrummed with life, soundtracked by incessant noise: touts, soi-dogs, and motorbikes. They weaved their way over the uneven pavement, through dense, sweating crowds, until they reached the entrance to their current haunt of choice. An elevator ride up sixty floors and they were in the clearer air of the sunset roof bar, Anika's eyes already scanning for likely targets. They took seats in a booth, ordered two waters, and waited. They never had to wait long. The whole routine made Millie uncomfortable, but as usual, she went along with it. If she didn't go, Anika might start bringing someone else. She might get *dumped.*

After a few minutes, a waiter approached. "Excuse me," he said, "The lady at the bar asked if she could join you."

He nodded in the woman's direction. She was exquisitely dressed in what Millie recognized to be expensive clothes, and what Anika said was a white Dior shirt dress. Millie cleared her throat nervously and looked to Anika for her judgment.

"I guess so," Anika said.

The woman introduced herself as Claudia. Her perfume was heady and sophisticated—sandalwood and smoke. She ordered cocktails for the three of them and asked the girls how long they'd been in the city, what their plans were, who they'd traveled with, reassuring them *how lovely it was* to chat. She was older than they were, perhaps by ten or even fifteen years, possessing a cool, seductive glamor. Anika did most of the talking, with Millie looking at her lap, offering the occasional word here or there.

"If you're struggling for money," said Claudia, taking an elegant drag from her cigarette, "I own a rambutan farm a bit farther down south that's always hiring. Easy work, lots of time to relax and take in the countryside, weekends at the beach…"

"We don't have work visas," said Anika.

Claudia scoffed and waved her hand. "You know, I'm not hitting on you, but you're really pretty. I mean *really* pretty."

Anika smiled.

"What's a rambutan?" asked Millie.

Anika glared at her, even though there was no way she was sure either. Claudia pulled out her phone and brought up some pictures of the exotic, red fruit.

"They look like testicles," said Millie.

"I don't know what testicles you've been looking at," said Anika.

"Not when they've got the skin on," she explained, pointing at a photo of the peeled fruit. "I've never even seen one before, have you?"

"A testicle?"

"No, a rambutan."

"Well, that's because all you eat is chips," snapped Anika.

"There's nothing in this world better or more valuable than a fresh, sweet rambutan," Claudia said with a smile. She patted Millie on the hand and looked deep into her eyes. "Believe me."

Millie excused herself to visit the bathroom. She splashed some water on her face and wondered if the time had come to throw in the towel and just go home. Perhaps she could borrow the money for the trip from someone and pay them back later. Maybe she didn't *need* to do this. As she considered, the door swung open, and a gaggle of long-legged girls poured in, laughing and fixing their faces together in the mirror.

Millie exited the bathroom and saw Anika and Claudia drawn in close, discussing something with serious expressions, though from across the bar, she couldn't tell what. She returned to the table, and the pair stopped talking abruptly. Claudia pulled her handbag closer and closed it, but not before Millie had spied a fat wad of cash inside.

"I think we're going to go to another bar," said Anika. She placed a hand on Millie's forearm, an unusual display of affection. "You're welcome to come along, obviously, but I told Claudia you're pretty tired tonight."

"Oh," said Millie. She felt tears pricking her eyes but smiled broadly. "Yeah, I might just head back, but you two go and have fun."

"Cool," said Anika.

Millie lay awake in the dark until 4:30 a.m., when Anika stumbled through the door and collapsed on her bed. For a moment, Millie pretended to be asleep, listening to the bang and clang of the all-night restaurant kitchen outside their window, and the periodic drunken laughter of passing tourists.

"Did you have a good time?" Millie finally asked.

"Yeah, it was fun."

"Did Claudia pay for everything?"

"Yep. Listen, I think I'm going to take her up on that rambutan farm job."

"I don't think we should go. We don't even know her." Millie said the words because she was *supposed* to say them. That was her role in this friendship: the boring, sensible downer.

"Don't go then," Anika barked. There was a pause. "Sorry," she said. "I didn't meant that."

Millie breathed. "I don't want us to fall out. We can do whatever you think is best."

"We'll go together. It'll be fine, it's just hot and late. Let's sleep."

LOADED LIKE CAMELS with their backpacks, they stood before the bustling entrance to the railway station, tucked into a shadowed corner to avoid the sun.

"Hi!" Claudia shouted, tottering forward in high heels. It had rained hard that morning and the floor was still slippery, making her gait awkward.

Millie couldn't help but think that the sunlight did Claudia no favors. She was distinctly less glamorous than she had been at the bar and somehow less secure in herself, as though the daytime hours undid her magic. She exchanged air kisses with Anika.

"Can I get a bit more information on where we're going?" said Millie.

"Ah, yes. So, you'll be on fruit-picking and sorting duty. There are a few other foreigners on the farm right now for you to meet. Lovely girls. It's 8,000 baht for a week's work.

You're going to catch the ten o'clock train and I've arranged for someone to pick you up on the other side. I'm so excited—you're going to love it!"

8,000 baht? It was almost too good to be true.

"But is there an address I can send to my parents?" Millie asked.

A micro-expression of embarrassment and annoyance flashed over Anika's face. She hated when Millie shattered the image of them being fully independent.

"Of course," said Claudia. "There's not an address as such, but it's a few miles from the train station. You'll be able to share your location once you arrive."

"We'll sort it all, don't worry," said Anika. "Don't tell our parents. You *know* how they'll react. They were bad enough when we told them we were going on that beach excursion. Besides, you're twenty-three. They don't need to know every detail of your life."

"Fine," said Millie.

The girls left Claudia, who stayed in the city to finish up some business. The train was already idling on the platform as they approached, and they boarded and found seats. Millie slumped against the hot glass of the window, wet with sweat, and mentally prepared to spend the next few hours in this boiling metal can. Pulling out of the station, she watched as they left the city behind. Anxiety bubbled in her stomach, and a dull ache throbbed in her arm.

"I hope this is a good idea," she said.

"It is," said Anika, not looking up while listlessly fanning herself with a leaflet.

The train chugged noisily through the beautiful Thai country-side. They passed towns and rural villages, dazzling expanses of lush greenery, swaying palms, and distant mountains. A man came through the carriage selling cold drinks, and they both bought one with the small amount of cash they still had. Then they fell back to silence, and Millie chewed at her fingernail and watched on her phone as the minutes and hours passed, taking her further and further from a place she could confidently navigate.

"I'm heading to the restroom," she said. Anika gave a perfunctory nod.

She made her way down the swaying aisle. The temperature in the bathroom stall was easily ninety degrees and required her to squat, so she decided not to go and instead to stretch her legs. As she did, the train pulled into a station. She looked out the window and she recognized the name on the sign. It was the stop just before theirs. She saw people getting off and heard the metallic drone of hidden cicadas.

She could get off here, too. Maybe she *should* get off. She hesitated. What would happen if she did? She could get a train back to Bangkok, probably, and then a flight home. There was nobody forcing her to go through with this. As the possibility buzzed in her mind, the train chugged to life once again and began to pull away.

What if Anika had had the same thought? What if Anika had *left her* and gotten off the train? In a panic, she rushed back down the now mostly empty aisle and was relieved to see her friend still sitting there.

Sunset rid the carriage of the worst of its heat, the blinding day giving way to a more peaceful evening. The train finally arrived at their destination, and the girls dragged their things onto the deserted platform.

"Thank God," said Anika. "That felt longer than the flight we took to get to Asia."

They heaved their luggage to the street outside, where a solitary car was waiting for them. The driver got out and began putting their things in the trunk. The girls climbed into the back, their sweaty legs sticking uncomfortably to the leather of the seats. Anika put a hand over her eyes and squinted.

"I've got a headache," she said. "I need to be quiet for a while."

"No worries," said Millie. "We'll be able to get water soon. You're probably just dehydrated."

The quiet, single-track lane took them past farms and fields. The night was upon them now, and each place they passed was deserted, almost pitch-black with the lack of street lamps. The farther they went, the more Millie's anxiety climbed. She jiggled her leg up and down rapidly.

"Will you stop that?" said Anika. "It's so annoying."

Millie leaned forward and spoke through the mesh that separated them from the driver. "Are we almost there?"

No reply.

"Excuse me," she said.

"He doesn't speak English. Can you be quiet? What are you so worried about?" said Anika.

Millie looked at her friend and felt she barely recognized her anymore, face obscured in the dark of the car. They continued for several minutes more before they reached what looked like a bus station. The car pulled over, and Anika frowned at Millie.

"Are we stopping for a toilet break?"

The driver left his seat and went around to Millie's side, opening her door. Without a word, she slid out. The driver closed the door behind her. Anika cocked her head like a confused dog and pulled at her own door handle but found it did nothing. She reached over to Millie's, but that, too, was useless. The doors could be opened only from the outside.

"I'm sorry," said Millie through the glass. "But you've been such a bitch recently, and after I got in touch with Claudia again, I couldn't say no."

Anika watched as the driver handed Millie a thick envelope. She looked baffled, like she was unable to fathom what was happening. Millie pushed the envelope inside her bag.

"What do you mean? What's happening?" said Anika, her voice muffled. "Is this a joke?"

"I've been to Thailand before, but you always forget that, don't you? It's always *you* that has to be in charge."

Millie began to walk away. An overnight bus and she'd be back on familiar turf.

Anika shouted her name. She banged on the window and pulled uselessly at her door handle, but she was trapped.

The driver climbed back into the front seat and restarted the engine.

"Let me out!" shouted Anika. "What's happening? I have to get out! Millie!"

The driver pulled out and down the road past the fields of rambutan.

SIMPLE LOYALTY

J. B. McLAURIN

WHEN I MET Jack, I knew he'd be a perfect fit. Just the right mix of confidence bordering on arrogance, a righteous hatred for his parents, and a desperate need to cut his own path. That lit tinderbox of pride and rebellion, I recognized it, because I'd had the same thing burning in me; it's why I cracked my mom over the head with her favorite rolling pin, then delivered a volley of fuck-you-blows for good measure—until she was spitting up teeth and blood but couldn't call me an idiot or a disappointment or blame me for the billionth time for my dad leaving. I'd set out for parts unknown at seventeen without a dollar to my name, right after leaving Mom bleeding and gasping on the linoleum floor. There were stumbles along the way, sure, but eventually I found my place. A community where simple loyalty was king.

I still feel that burn though. It crackles through me sometimes, hungry.

It's like a wild fire, you know, that need to rebel and live apart.

I guess if you're not careful though, it can burn everything right up.

HE WAS SITTING and sipping coffee in Malaprops bookstore in Asheville, reading some dense book about the fall of the Romanov Dynasty. That was about the only store I went into downtown. I'd go and scan the aisles, grab some books for me, some special requests for my neighbors, maybe a coffee, then leave. That day, I decided to stay. Jack acted like he was interested in what I was reading and we started talking.

We met again the following week even though it had to be planned down to the minute because I didn't carry a phone, which he couldn't stop obsessing over.

A few nights later, over far too many craft beers, we talked about life and the sad state of our society. I went back to his place and stayed the night.

And that became our routine: books and beers and drunken sex that always steered into conversations about how we both wanted something different out of life. How we didn't want to clock in and out. How we didn't want to pay a mortgage and taxes and a cell phone bill. How we didn't want to go to church and drop our kids off at school-band practice.

We were destined for something more. We didn't want to be just some ants marching to the humdrum tune of conformity.

In short, like me, Jack didn't want to play it safe.

Finally, one day he said: *I want to see your place, Jessie.*

"JESUS CHRIST, I can't believe what I'm seeing. Who built all these?" He asked, full of wonder. We were walking the grounds of the community.

"Not sure, exactly. Everyone says Ron Holbrook, this old hippie who was one of the first people here. He came up with the plans and along with some others, built them back in the seventies."

A series of cabins curved around like a horseshoe; in the middle, a pond glistened with sunlight. Men and women were gathered at its bank chatting, feet in the water. All around, the place hummed with activity: people cooking, cleaning, gathering in groups to wax philosophical, dogs scampering about.

Jack commented that the place was like some pre-colonial village of settlers. Sure, people had contemporary clothes, but he couldn't get over how there wasn't a modern amenity in sight.

"And it's been around," I said, "kind of like a secret, since then. We keep to ourselves and try not to mix too much with people in town."

He grinned. "Well, what about me? Aren't you breaking the rules?"

"We make the occasional exception." I grabbed him, tugged him down to my height, and kissed him. Then we kept walking.

"Jesus, you've been here for thirteen years, you said?" he asked.

"Give or take."

"What about winters? It must be unbearable."

I pointed to the black chimneys jutting out of the cabins. "They all have stove fireplaces to keep them toasty. We get by just fine, don't worry."

"Where's yours?"

I pointed at the horseshoe's bend. Our cabins had tidy front porches for sitting, reading, and leaning over the rail to catch up with neighbors.

We walked over to my humble abode and went right in. The giddiness of the moment swept over Jack; he picked me up and took me right to the bed.

In the afterglow, we lazed around, messy sheets barely covering our bodies.

Caressing my arm, he mused, "I didn't quite picture it this way. But I've always wanted to be involved in something unique. I know it sounds weird, but living like this, it's like the real version of punk rock. It's not just saying it or screaming it in a song. This is really living it."

Jack was a full-time musician, gigging around Asheville most nights, and barely scraping by. He was a bartender on the side, too. But he didn't drink much, thankfully, and he kept in really good shape.

"Don't take yourself too seriously there, Jacky," I said playfully and kissed him on the shoulder.

He smiled, but then suddenly frowned.

"What?" I asked. He waved me off. "No, come on, what's bothering you?"

"I want to be a part of something like this..." he trailed off.

"But…? Come on, since when have you been shy?"

"I don't want to join a cult."

I shot up, covers sliding off. "That's what you think we are? Bunch a crazies living in the woods sacrificing animals and performing rituals or some shit?"

He propped himself up. "No, no. That's not what I meant. It's just, I'm an atheist. This isn't like a religious thing, is it? Like a fundamentalist cul—" he stopped, rightfully guessing that word would have sent me into overdrive.

"We're not a cult, Jack. We're a community. We take care of each other and live quiet lives. This isn't about some charismatic leader we think is the second coming, or seances or any other crazy shit. It's simply about community."

"You're serious?"

"Why would I lie to you?" I said, voice cracking, revealing my vulnerability. I saw a future with him in this cabin. Late nights with hearty meals and reading in front of the fire, snuggling on the couch, owls providing a spooky backwoods score. "I want you here with me."

"You're not messing with me?"

"I wouldn't have brought you out here if I wasn't serious."

Jack was only the third outsider I'd ever brought. The rules were pretty damn strict, but we could get to all that later. All that fine print might spoil the deal. Plus, I was pretty confident the hook had been set.

"And this place isn't about religion?"

"Jesus, how many more times do I have to say it? It's not about a messiah. It's not about catching a ride on a comet or mass suicide. I told you. We check in on each other. Like it's supposed to be. Like you said, this place is like punk rock in action. Well, we're a community in action."

"Okay, okay. I hear you." He got closer to me and I straddled him. We kissed, slow, soft.

I wanted him here. I really did.

I KNEW TODAY was going to be tough for Jack, so I let him sleep in. I brewed a heaping pot of coffee and made breakfast with all the fixings. He was going to need it.

"Hey, babe. Morning," he said, rubbing his face.

"Come on over. I've got a spread for you."

He joined me at my breakfast table. The window over it gave us a view of Horseshoe Bend, my nickname for our community. We had no official name for it. Some people called it the Outpost. Others, The Camp or Emerald City.

The sun was up. People were milling about. Clanking gardening tools and murmuring voices came through the cracked window.

I'd already checked in with the others before Jack got up. They were ready to go and just as nervous as me. This part was always the hardest. I didn't want to eat beforehand. The other times I'd gotten sick out in the woods. Best to do this on an empty stomach.

The meeting was in an hour. He needed to eat up, then start hydrating.

"Go ahead. Eat, eat."

"Okay, okay." He grabbed his fork and started champing down. "What are we doing today? Heading back to town? I was supposed to work but I can call in sick."

"You should do that," I said. He nodded. "And we can head back into town later for you to get your things."

It was a gamble saying this, but I knew it was a safe one. The hook was indeed set and couldn't be ripped out of his lip with pliers.

"Wait, you already want me to move in? Tonight?"

"You getting cold feet on me?"

He grinned. "Tonight it is, then." He ate more, gobbling down my famous hashbrowns and raving about how delicious they were. I never skimped with the butter. That was the secret. "Why can't we just head back and get my stuff now?"

"There's something you have to do first."

"WHERE ARE WE going?" Jack asked.

"It's just ahead," I said, pointing to the clearing. Jack had been a good solider thus far, not questioning why two of my friends, Mallory and Eric, along with other outsiders, were hiking with us.

Summer was edging into fall; the leaves hadn't started turning yet. The temperature was in the seventies, which would give him a better chance of making it. Dehydration had gotten the better of the last man I recruited.

The group stopped when we reached the clearing. I steered Jack over to the edge of the cliff and, despite his anxious interruptions, started explaining the test.

"You see that trail over there." I pointed at a rocky path leading down into the gulley. It was the only way to get down from the cliff without plunging into pine trees that would leave you hanging like meat on a skewer. "That's where you'll walk down."

"What the hell are you talking about? I'm done with this hike. Let's head back."

I grabbed him by both sides of his face as hard as I could. "You need to listen, because you have to do this."

He shook his head, wide-eyed, looking at me as if I'd lost my mind. "Are you okay?"

"I'm not screwing around. You just have to make it to the other side of the gulch." Which was about four, maybe five miles across, but full of some pretty inhospitable terrain. It was true wilderness and it didn't give one shit about your survival. "There are paths on the other side that lead to the marked tree. You have to make it to the marked tree. It's got an owl carved into it. You can't miss it. That's the finish line."

"The marked tree? An owl? Jesus, Jessie, listen to yourself. You sound crazy. Let's just go back and have lunch and then leave."

I pulled him even further aside. I didn't want the others eavesdropping. Plus, I didn't want them looking at my hands. As I pulled Jack away, I stole glances at the others: Eric and Mallory were prepping their respective candidates—a middle-aged man, who was a little soft around the waistline and likely didn't stand a chance, and a twenty-something woman with the trim figure of a mountain climber, who probably had the best odds of making it.

"Listen to me. This is real and it's about to start. Here, take this." I'd never put my thumb on the scale before, let alone engaged in full-blown cheating. But I desperately wanted a life with Jack out here in the pines. So, I shoved the tactical knife into his pocket. Meanwhile, his eyes started cutting around in all directions as if looking for a means of escape.

"Don't try and run away," I warned. "That won't end well."

"What the fuck, Jessie? Are you threatening me?"

"It's not a threat. It's just the truth. Don't try to escape. Mallory and Eric won't stand for it. No one can know about this place."

He got in my face, nose to nose. "And what will you do if I run, huh?"

"Don't put me in that position." I pulled him in for a kiss; he reluctantly complied. "I don't want to hurt you."

"Hurt me? Okay, screw this—" Jack turned and started sprinting back down the trail.

The hurried clomp of his boots alerted Mallory. She quickly unshouldered her pack and pulled out the case to her crossbow. A novice couldn't unpack and load it in time. But Mallory was a prodigy with a bow.

Jack had made it about twenty yards when she let the first arrow fly. It speared a pine just to his left, and he stopped cold.

Mallory screamed, "You take another step toward camp and the next one goes in your back." She'd already nocked another arrow.

I yelled, trying to make my voice as soothing as possible, but probably failing. "Come back, babe. All you have to do is make it across. It's that simple."

Reluctantly, Jack returned to us. Then I began explaining the rules to him and the other outsiders. As I spoke, they trembled and shot disbelieving glances at each other. "In the end, all you have to do to be a part of this community is to take a simple test of loyalty. We have to know you're serious about being part of what we have together here. That you'd be willing to risk your life at the drop of hat if we asked you. You make it across and touch that tree and you're one of us."

"Oh, so if we just participate in your little *Hunger Games* test, then we get to live? Swell," Jack remarked snidely, staring at me like I was fit for an asylum. I had no clue what the *Hunger Games* was.

"You can't help each other. You have to separate and go at it on your own. And there's no time limit, once—"

"So that's it," Jack interrupted. "We just make it to the other side and we're good?"

It seemed he'd accepted his circumstances. Like maybe it wasn't going to be that bad.

I had to burst his bubble. Nothing was that easy.

"No baby, we're going to hunt you."

Jack looked at me as if I'd just told him I was a Martian.

Behind me, Mallory finished loading our crossbows. Rifles were unfair to the candidates, but a bow gave them a fighting chance. After all, we wanted these people here with us. No one took pleasure in catching and killing them. But they had to want the life. We couldn't manufacture that desire for them. And we couldn't take them at their word that they'd be loyal: They had to demonstrate it.

Mallory passed out our respective weapons, then we each bid our candidate farewell.

"You can do this," I reassured him. "Just keep your head down and don't stop moving."

"This is insane, Jessie. You're all fucking crazy."

His words shredded me. But it was okay; it was just the nerves talking. He didn't mean it.

"You run thirty miles a week, babe." One of the many reasons I chose him. Bringing an overweight smoker out here was a surefire way to find yourself burying a body at dusk. "You've got this."

I kissed him and backed away, then yelled, "Go!"

At first, none of them took off. This was typical—well, typical in the context of the times we'd tried this, which was once every four years out of necessity: Too many disappearances led to too many questions.

Eric pulled out a small revolver—one of only a handful of firearms in the camp, save for the shotguns and rifles we used for hunting wild game. He fired a warning shot into the air and another into the dirt.

That got everyone moving.

We always gave them an hour-long head-start, so we settled in to watch them scurry down the mountain. Initially, they tried to stay together, but Eric fired another shot and yelled, "Split up or we'll come for you right now."

They complied.

I watched Jack break ahead of the group. His long gazelle-like legs propelled him through the woods. He was going to make it. I just knew it.

But I still dreaded what lay ahead. Once I was down there, I couldn't give him a break. I'd hunt the others first like I always did. But I had to honor my pledge to the community: I had to hunt every candidate down in the gulch. Even the one I brought.

Two hours went by, all three still alive, but the middle-aged man was flagging. Eric had brought him. Before everything got started, I'd watched Eric give him a hug and a passionate kiss for encouragement while the poor guy sobbed. None of us had the heart to hunt *our* candidates right out of the gate, so we'd randomly split off and hunt the others. Eric was after Mallory's woman and Mallory was hot after Jack. But Jack had a good lead on her. Problem was, Mallory was one of the best hunters we had. Jack couldn't break pace—not for a second—if he wanted to beat her.

Eric's candidate was just ahead, beyond some trees, tiptoeing across a dry creek bed of jagged rocks and boulders. He was using his arms for balance, like he was walking on a high wire. I slowed down to give him a chance. I didn't mind skirting my oath, sort of like a lawyer bending words. But once I reached the opening, I knew I'd have to take the shot.

Next, I heard the sandpaper-scuff of boots on rock.

I ran to the creek bed and found him.

He'd lost balance and fallen face-first into a jagged rock; it had caved-in his face and bulldozed right through his skull, turning his brain to mush.

Another hour passed. I caught up to Eric and delivered the bad news. He sunk to his knees, threw his crossbow aside and wept. I left him to grieve.

About a hundred yards later, as I drew closer to the other side, I saw the woman charging up the trail. She was about twenty yards away from the marked tree.

I stopped and nocked an arrow, then I sighted her and let loose.

The arrow gouged right through her leg. Arrowhead on one side and fletching on the other. She wailed and screamed, but she was a tough one. She kept going and collapsed against the tree, wood-engraved owl resting just above her head.

Good for her, I thought. I'll make her dinner tonight.

Where is Mallory? I thought next. Better yet, where's Jack?

Branches rustled not far to my left. Unlike the other side of the gulch, this one had companion trails leading up to the cliff's edge, all of which guided the victor home to the owl.

I jogged to the left, dreading finding Mallory alone or worse, Jack struggling to get up the hillside.

When I got there, my worst fear was realized. Jack was there, limping up the trail.

But he was alone. And he hadn't seen or heard me yet.

I could just let him go. Mallory wasn't here and Eric was two miles back. Who would know?

"I'm too weak to take the shot." Mallory's pained voice cracked behind me. I turned to see her walking up to me. So much for mercy. "He had a knife. How'd he get a knife?" she asked, genuinely confused, while I thanked the gods she didn't suspect me of cheating.

Shoulder to shoulder with me, holding her wounded flank, she placed a sympathetic hand on my forearm and whispered, "You have to. It's the oath we all took. If we break it, then—"

"I know. I know."

This place had brought me peace, turning the wildfire inside me into a controlled burn. If I didn't honor my loyalty pledge to our community, then I would undo all I'd gained.

Plus, with Mallory watching, I couldn't throw the shot. I had to aim true.

He'd reached the top of the trail, still unaware of our presence.

I exhaled and let the arrow fly. I'd been true to my oath and led him like a good hunter always does—anticipating where the prey will be, not where it is—and the arrow slid through the middle of his back. The blow stunned him; he turned in shock, arrowhead poking through his chest like a bloody weathervane. Then he fell down and I couldn't see him.

I left Mallory and ran up to him.

When I got there, he was gasping and rolling on the ground.

I bent down and wiped the hair from his face. Told him to get up, even though I knew he was done. God, how I wished he'd just stand up and walk over to that tree.

He met my gaze, a potent blend of fear and anger churning in his eyes. "You're fucking crazy, you know that? You're a monster. You're going to get caught. The police—"

I put my hand over his blood-specked mouth and pressed the index finger of my other hand against my lips. "You don't mean that, Jack," I said. "What we had was real."

I took my hand off his mouth, hoping in vain we could enjoy our last moments together.

He mumbled something I didn't understand, then went still.

SIMON SAYS

FRANCES HOPE

I'M HONESTLY SURPRISED Mom never tried making us sick. It was the next logical step when the attention started to wane, but I guess she just didn't think of it. I know she had the stomach for it.

A doctor extricated me from my mother's womb on March 5, 2009, after a grueling seventeen-hour labor in which I refused to come out of my own accord. That's what Mom told me, anyway. Her obsession with documentation only started somewhere around two months postpartum, so I don't have any photo or video content to confirm my birth story. But I'll give her that one. Among all her faults, dishonesty isn't high on the list.

My gram, Mom's mom, was a raging narcissist. My uncle, Mom's brother, was the golden child, and my mom *just had to accept* her unimportance. I had sympathy for Mom once, but that dried up when she made me lose my last friend a few months ago.

"Your mom's too weird, I can't deal!" Emily had said. We weren't *best* friends or anything, but we did hang out. Emily had a reputation for being sweet, and I thought I'd be safe from a confrontation like this.

"I don't have any control over her," I'd tried to explain, almost crying but holding on to my last little bit of dignity. "She's always been like . . . *this*." I gestured in my mom's direction, where she was leaning against the side of our truck, waiting for me. Could she hear me? Did I care?

I ran a hand through my golden hair, fingering the dyed-purple ends that I'd stupidly thought might set me apart. Out of the corner of my eye, I saw Mom smooth down her own golden tresses and play with her own dyed-purple ends. It had taken her one day to catch up. That had been a good day.

"Simon says dye your hair," I muttered to myself.

Emily stared at me, biting her lip.

"And you're weird too," she said finally, then turned and walked off.

Turns out Emily was a real bitch.

My mom was normal at first, if the smattering of photos and short videos from the first weeks of my infancy meant anything. And my dad was still around then too, though even in those early photos you can see that he and Mom didn't have the foundation of closeness they would have needed to withstand Mom's crazy. There isn't a single photo of them together with me. Then again, maybe Gram just never offered to take family photos, and Mom was well trained by that point not to ask her for anything.

My mom thought Gram would treat me the way she'd treated her, and save any grandparental love for the golden child's future firstborn. But Gram was *enamored* with me in a way that I think—and I've had a lot of time to think, in my social isolation—probably delighted my mom at first but later destroyed her.

It might have been easier if Mom had just resented me like any sensible parent would, but instead, she started to *become* me. Matching outfits for parent and baby on certain occasions are fine, like the coordinated, full-body Christmas jammies so many stores shove down our throats starting the day after Halloween. I feel sick whenever I see ads for those things because that's been my life every hour, every day since before I can remember.

Of course she couldn't stop at just the matching outfits. The endless photos of us looking like asynchronous twins soon turned into endless videos. Mom on her back next to me, kicking her legs in the air. Mom crawling around our thick-pile living room rug. She was there for all the milestones.

Who knows what Mom thought her behavior would do for her relationship with her mother. My uncle, Gram's original golden child, had a kid when I was two and a half, siphoning my grandmother to their house. I'm sure what was happening in ours repulsed her. Any cuteness in me had to have been sullied by the grown woman aping my every move.

My dad stuck it out till I was four, just old enough for me to remember a sound bite from their last fight.

"You are actually *sick*, Deena," he said.

I remember thinking, *My mom's not sick.* I didn't know "sick" could mean unwell in the head. Just like I didn't know that my dad left us because of my mom, and not because of something I did. And I didn't know that it wasn't normal, having millions of internet strangers watch and rewatch the videos my mom constantly posted.

Now that I'm older, I've looked at some of the comments people left on those videos through the years. They started off thinking we had a cute little mommy-daughter thing going. Then they thought it was satire. Then people caught on that my mom was just insane. We were even featured on a few daytime talk shows, right alongside the surprise paternity test results, the twins dating the same man, and the addicts there to tell stories of redemption who'd been liquored up by producers backstage to make for better TV.

I was too young to understand that we were part of a modern-day freak show, the viewers trading carnival stalls for glowing laptop and television screens. My mom should have known, but she didn't care. What mattered to her, I can only assume, is that eyes were on us. She was finally getting that precious attention she'd always wanted.

Back then, I wished I could be enough for her, that my attention and love could fill her up and make her whole. Over time, that wish transformed into a desperate desire for her to just be normal like the other moms. Now all I want is for her to stay as far away from me as possible, but I'm scared that she thinks she *is* me.

It's a miracle she didn't homeschool me. My best guess is

that she needed me to be *somewhere*, nowhere too fun, while she passed the time at her office job and probably fantasized about being a student herself. When I got my first boyfriend at twelve, a cute guy whose family was from Spain, guess who got a boyfriend no more than two weeks later? She settled for a French guy who walked out of her life just about as fast as he entered it. She flaunted him embarrassingly enough to drive my own boyfriend away, though, so we got dumped around the same time. Twins!

Those aren't the only unhinged things she did. There were plenty of others that make me blush, cry, gag, scream even to think about them. I snapped at my mom the night after Emily dumped me as a friend. It wasn't the first time I yelled at her, but I must have caught her at a bad moment.

"You are such a *freak*, Mom," I shrieked, wanting to punch her or punch a wall, anything to get the rage out of my body.

She slapped me hard across the face. She'd never hit me before, and I felt a tingly heat where her skin had met mine. After she did it, she just stood there for a moment, face blank, arms at her sides, watching me, not saying a word.

Then she slapped her own face with the opposite hand, just as hard as she had mine. She turned and walked away.

I DABBLED IN making my own online content a couple of years ago, just the occasional lip-synching video, me hugging the cat, a little social commentary, whatever. For a blissful week, Mom didn't realize what I was doing. It felt *so good* getting attention just for me, and because I'd changed schools thanks to a cross-town move, the classmates who saw and complimented my stuff didn't know my story yet. Then, of course, my mom found the videos, started making her own copycat content, linked to mine, and before I had even been in school long enough to learn which bathroom stalls were the grossest and which teachers let you get away with late homework, I was the weird kid with the weird mom all over again.

I recently had an idea for some new content, though. It came to me the night my mom slapped me, as I was sitting at the little desk in my bedroom and staring into space when I should have been doing my math homework. The red mark on my cheek had faded, but my face remembered how her hand felt when it made contact.

I pulled out a blank notebook from my drawer, a journal with a pretty cover that had been too pristine to write in until now. The whole plan didn't come to me at once, just the start, and I didn't let my mind travel to where the idea might lead.

On the page, I laid out the following, taking inspiration from the lab report I'd just handed in for science class:

EXPERIMENT #1: SKIN RASH

Date today: 11/8/24

Planned action date: 11/9/24

Possible risks: Might damage skin permanently? (probably not)

Materials needed: 3–4 spicy peppers, knife

Method: Place cut peppers on arms to make red patches

Desired results: Appearance of eczema or other skin rash

Results:

I didn't know whether my experiment would work, but I had an idea that it would, just based on the way my hands had burned for hours after cutting a jalapeño for my mom to put in guacamole.

As it turned out, the pain was worth the payoff. My arms looked terrible, and they stung enough that I could cry tears of despair over my "eczema" despite my lack of any notable acting talent. The video I posted of my suffering online got my peers' attention. Even if they were hate-watching, I know they saw it, shared it, and would be eager for more.

Did Mom read my journal? I don't think so, because she didn't seem to know how to re-create the red patches on her own skin. Once she noticed my arms, though, she cooed over them, so motherly, soothing my skin with aloe and bandaging my arms. I'm sure the bandages were just so she could copy my look.

Did Mom see my video? Definitely. A day after I'd posted mine, she starred in her own, all gauze-covered arms and tears about the skin condition she and her daughter shared.

It was so embarrassing—*excruciating*—knowing that strangers, peers, and my former friends were watching our videos side-by-side and laughing at her. At us, let's be honest. But no pain, no gain, right?

Three days after the experiment, two days after I posted my video, and one day after Mom made and shared hers, I completed my experiment report:

Results: Arms looked patchy and stung a lot; success

FOR THE SECOND and third experiments, I continued with skin conditions, each time similarly documenting my procedure and the anticipated risks of the experiment. Different materials, different results, same risk-reward payoff. These were still low-risk experiments anyway, and I was careful to do some online research, always with the browser in private mode, to get a good sense of what would happen to me each time. I logged the results once I had them.

I don't think she realized until Experiment #3 that I was doing this to myself. My journal—closed, it's not like I was broadcasting my experimental procedure to the world or anything—appeared in the bottom-left corner of my second video when I was giving a gruesome close-up of the peeling skin on the back of my hand. My mom probably hated that I could lift off my bandages and show some gore, when she had to keep her bandages on.

But I think that seeing the journal in the frame, even if she didn't register it at the time, must have made her notice it on my desk the next time she snooped in my room. She might not have thought to open it if the video hadn't foreshadowed its importance.

She never told me she found the journal, but I knew she had when I saw the same bottle of extra-strength hair bleach on her sink that I had purchased for my third skin condition. She wasn't the only one who knew how to snoop. My journal entry for Experiment #3 was written on 12/2/24, with a planned action date of 12/4/24. She had the bleach on 12/3/24, ready to carry out my private experiment on herself.

Simon says wreck your skin.

This time our skin conditions appeared on the same day, hers a little before mine, and our videos were posted within a few hours of each other. She didn't give me bandages this time, and she didn't use any herself.

If she knew I was harming myself like this, why didn't she stop me? Well, these were still low-risk experiments, I thought to myself. There was still time for Mom to intervene.

It probably pissed her off that my third video was my last. But she couldn't say anything, really, without admitting to me that she knew what I'd been up to and admitting to herself what *she'd* been up to. Maybe she hoped I'd start up the videos again in time.

I was done making online content, but I didn't stop the experiments, and neither did Mom.

Simon says vomit a couple times.

Simon says lose your hair.

Simon says puke for twenty-four hours and become dehydrated.

We actually went to the doctor for the twenty-four-hour one, Experiment #6.

"We think we got food poisoning," Mom said to the ER triage nurse, smiling weakly through a stomach cramp.

I hated hearing the word "we" come out of her mouth.

They had us in different rooms, slated to receive IV fluids and monitoring, but my mom video-called me once she was alone.

"Isn't this terrible, honey?" she said, like we hadn't just done this to ourselves. "Everyone has to make such a fuss over us."

"Yeah, Mom, it's so terrible," I said.

I couldn't be sure since I wasn't in the room with her, but she looked like she was *trembling* with the excitement of it all. She was loving every second of our shared ER visit, and I just knew that if she'd experimented with making me sick herself when I was a kid, I'd be dead and scattered by now.

When we were finally discharged, after the relatively mild toxin we gave ourselves had worked its way through our systems undetected by medical staff, the first thing I did was update my journal on the outcome of Experiment #6:

> **Results:** Vomiting and dehydration requiring ER visit; success

I KEPT AT my experiments for four months, taking occasional breaks when my body needed them. I did my due diligence each time to make sure I wasn't going to accidentally kill myself, and I always documented the risk level.

I put myself through hell, which meant my mom went through it too. But I hadn't *made* her watch my videos or find my journal. I never made her do anything she didn't want to do. And unlike her, I took no pleasure in it.

One more, I told myself. *Then I'm done.*

EXPERIMENT #11: THE BIG ONE

Date today: 3/8/25

Planned action date: 3/11/25

Possible risks: Death

I took a deep, shaky breath as I filled out the rest of the experiment sheet. Drain cleaner was the first material needed, but there were a few equally nasty others.

I left a bigger gap this time between the date I wrote down Experiment #11 and the planned execution date, because gathering the materials might take some effort, and we didn't have most of them in the house.

I wondered, right up until the day of the experiment, if this would be the one where my mom would stop me. Did she even care if I died, chemical-burned from the inside? Even with everything she'd done to me over the years, I still cried when I saw the bag, hidden behind her bathroom sink, full of supplies for Experiment #11. She was okay with the risk for herself, and she was okay with it for me.

I hate her. I don't understand her. I know that she's needed help for a long time. Having the capacity for empathy makes this more painful than if I were a sociopath or a narcissist or whatever I'd have to be for it not to feel terrible, this thing I need to do.

There were many, many times when I wanted my mom to stop the grotesque mimicry, to just let me be a person without a disgusting shadow always beside me. But this time, I'm counting on her to do it once more.

Of course she will.

I rip my eleven pages of experiments into pieces and flush them down the toilet. The only thing any investigators will find, when they come, is my mom's body and a receipt for a purchase she made yesterday afternoon, along with some partially empty containers of very harsh but readily available household chemicals.

I didn't buy any, because I won't be performing Experiment #11 on myself. Not today, not ever.

MUSCLE WATER

MICHAEL A. REED

THE JUNIOR VARSITY football team, the coaches and the scrawny boys pretending to be men watch suspiciously as I pour a cup of vapor-distilled Muscle Water. I swish the cup in circles over the boys' heads as if ordaining them for the great work of the jungle. I don't spill a precious drop.

"In my hand, I hold the perfect stabilized blend of palpable hydration," I announce. "Designed for an active lifestyle and saturated with the richest minerals, Muscle Water is the healthiest, most well-rounded performance water on the market."

Believe in magic. Believe in me. Believe in your thirst.

I drink.

They lean closer.

"Watch me," I say as I take up the hundred-pound dumbbell and curl it. My veins pop in my forearm and my bicep groans with unimaginable strength. I'm no longer the flimsy middle-aged loser that entered their weight room to sell overpriced sports liquids. I'm a lion, a god.

Hollering and cheering, the team launches to their feet and roars with me. They witness my hidden potential, my raw energy dripping from the sweat of my brow. They fumble with their phones, finally caring enough to take a video. I'm too wild to ignore now. I'm too beast.

The coaches don't regret inviting me to conduct a product showcase anymore. They've never seen their players so hyped.

All thanks to the undeniable potency of Muscle Water. My holy grail.

Believe in me. Believe in your thirst.

I leap and I yell and exemplify incredible balance. I'm a cat in the tree, its tail dangling, flicking like a beckoning finger. Come on, boys. Drink up. Put your mouths in the lagoon and become the gators looking back at you.

I scan for a participant in order to fully convince the crowd. My rabbit in the hat. A weak link. The final line of proof that Muscle Water will change not just their athletic performance, but their very lives.

He stands at the back of the pack, his eyes eager, his stare unblinking. From a single glance, I know he is the perfect lamb for my table. His arms are thin, the elbows knobby, the shoulders shallow. Freckles mark his baby-boy face. He isn't made for football. For sports. For anything. The glasses give him away. The way he pushes them up his nose. The fact that he sweats without moving, uncomfortable in his own skin.

"Come on up, young man!" I shout, pointing to the fragile boy.

Everyone laughs, of course. They don't think that Muscle Water can alter the bottom of the food chain. But they will witness the truth.

"What's your name?" I ask once the boy is standing in front of me.

He can hardly look me in the eye when he answers, "Jackson, sir."

I pour a fresh cup of Muscle Water and hand it to Jackson. He takes it sheepishly, afraid to crumple the cheap paper and spill the sample of life-saving water.

"There's only one secret," I whisper into his ear. "Do you want to know what it is?"

Jackson gazes up at me, the peach fuzz on his lip trembling with anticipation. There is a dream trapped in his throat. A savage need to perform in the iron-boy circus, to compete in this measurement of manhood.

He probably soothes his ego with the usual lies: *Sports aren't really my thing. I want to focus on academics. I didn't know I had exercise-induced asthma.* Except, what he really wants is plain to see. He wants to be stronger than other boys. He wants to be faster, too. Domination. Oppression. Satisfaction.

He is me, decades younger, and drying on the vine. And I will quench his desire.

"Believe in the animal that you are, Jackson," I conclude.

Hesitant, he downs the Muscle Water. He doesn't look different. I doubt he feels different. It hasn't done the good work, yet.

I place the dumbbell in front of Jackson's feet. I suspect it's at least six times heavier than he has ever lifted. In fact, it may weigh more than his entire brittle body. Any other boy would've given up before they even tried. It is impossible, after all. Except, I saw the way he watched me lift. I saw the hope swirling in those pale blue eyes.

Jackson leans down. He wraps his spaghetti fingers around the dumbbell. His teammates jeer and video-record his feeble shell of bone and flesh. To them, he is no more powerful than wet tissue, tattered and strewn on the bathroom floor.

Until Jackson lifts the dumbbell.

He screams. Spit torpedoes from between his chapped lips as his face darkens. The hundred-pound weight rises slowly toward him like an inevitable future. His muscles creak. His eyes glow with the truth once he has the dumbbell above his waist. He is a man. He is a creature. He is strong. He is a believer. He is fire. He is the chill in the room.

For the first time in his life, Jackson's teammates celebrate his achievements. They fist bump him, slap his butt, and shake his shoulders. It is everything he ever wanted and more. He has earned his spot in the pride.

AFTER THE SESSION, I sell dozens of Muscle Water crates to the boys and discuss sponsorship deals with the coaches. I'm exhausted but try not to let it show.

Side effects don't make money.

On the surface, Muscle Water is just vitamin-enriched supplements, sustainable and responsibly harvested. Energy-infused aquifer water drawn from the long untapped wells beneath Montana's mountains.

But beneath the surface, there is another layer of animalism bubbling in its depths (…and perhaps a touch of lab-enhanced male hormones).

Jackson stays behind once everyone else has gone.

"I can't afford to buy any Muscle Water," he says. From the way his voice cracks, I realize he is tired, like me. The magic of the water touched his cells in the same way they touched mine. It worked, and now he wants more.

"I'll give you it for free," I say to my new water sommelier. I can't let the beast in him fade. It would be an injustice to the product—and the boy. The prey deserves to become the predator at some point in his life, and Jackson's time has arrived.

Together, Jackson and I walk to the parking lot where his mother waits for him, her arms folded and her eyes narrowed.

"Where have you been?" she asks.

She points to a mountain of boxed snacks and power drinks that appear to be left over from the school's snack-shack sales. I examine Jackson' mother and immediately recognize her breed. She is a zealous PTA member and queen of football game ticket admissions. Nobody gets into those bleachers without a proper school ID. No unauthorized food or drink. Hoodies down. Pants pulled up.

It's clear to me that Jackson's mom is part of his weakness.

"Go ahead, Jackson," I say, uncapping a warm bottle of Muscle Water. "Show your mom what you can do."

Jackson downs the bottle like a starving newborn. I drink my own bottle. Together, we are twin wolves, snarling and gurgling and barking. We are made for lifting boxes of snacks into the back of minivans. Niacin. Pantothenic acid. Amino proteins. Potassium. We become the vitamins that invigorate our blood, and we chuck the snacks to each other like a line of grizzled coal miners culling the earth of its sweet energy.

"Strong!" I shout as I manhandle a half-empty box of honey buns.

"Fast!" Jackson yells, his arms shaking beneath the weight of a dozen Gatorade packages.

We are in step with each other. Kindred spirits chasing the wind through tips of Savannah grass, longing for relevance in the midst of a boring existence. Jackson smiles at me. I smile back. Our sweat droplets form lakes of pure adrenaline on the hot asphalt.

Believe in your thirst. Believe in me. Believe in Jackson.

It doesn't take long to pack the minivan's trunk. The entire time, Jackson's mom stands aside, her mouth ajar and her car keys, littered with Disney keychains and supermarket loyalty cards, hanging by the tip of her finger. Mind blown, she witnesses a miracle of nature: the boy she once called Jackson.

I high five Jackson, and we revel in the audible clap that echoes across the parking lot. I flex my bicep and run my finger along the vein. Jackson flexes, too, his own muscles more defined than they had been an hour before.

"What the hell?" Jackson's mom exclaims when she steps closer to the trunk.

She points to the disaster in her trunk, a heap of trashed snack bags and uncapped drinks spilling into the fiber of the vehicle's carpet. "What is wrong with you?" She looks at me with disgust. "Who even are you?"

"Muscle Water sales consultant," I say, still catching my breath.

"It's amazing what Muscle Water can do," Jackson says in my defense. "I might make the team this year… I will make the team."

Jackson's mother turns red. She begins to unpack the trunk, muttering curse words under her breath.

"Stop," Jackson demands. He tries to put the snacks back, but his mother swats his hand away.

"We'll talk when we get home," his mother says, refusing to look at him. "And you!" She jabs a finger in the air and aims it at me. "I'll be calling the school administration to discuss your presence on campus." She smirks and winds up the killing blow. "You shouldn't be here. You clearly shouldn't be allowed around kids."

All the while, Jackson's anger erupts across his skin. His arm hair erects, and his jaw tightens. Any words he should say are drowned behind the saliva caulking his gums.

The boy will defend the leader of his pack. He will prove his place in the clan of man-turned-creatures and embrace the sheer vigor of zero calories, effervescent bubbles, and natural flavors.

Jackson's mother doesn't notice. She turns to me, hands on her hips. "Don't make me call the police."

When the final word of the threat leaves her mouth, Jackson shoves his mother into the side of the car. She falls to the pavement, her keys flying, her discount sunglasses tumbling, her gas station t-shirt riding up her stomach.

"Mommy?" Jackson asks, his face draining of color, eyes wide with horror.

Her only answer is the way she stares up at him from the ground. Disappointed. Disgusted. It is a look Jackson's mother must have been brewing in the back of her mind or practicing in the mirror each morning that he went to school. It is a trained and measured flat line. The point from A to B. From birth until now. Further proof that she and her son are not the same species.

Quietly, she begins to cry. And it cuts Jackson clean open.

His juiced physique fades away and the would-be-man in him melts at the sight of his mother leaning against the bald car tire. He is no beast. He is no predator. Unable to separate who he is from what he was, Jackson sobs, his snot dribbling down his chin. For a moment, he exists outside the lines of his body, the ghost of an animal hunted to extinction.

"I'm sorry," Jackson whispers. I'm so sorry, Mom."

I won't let him disappear that easily, though.

Jackson kneels beside his mother, but I pull him away. "You went too far," I say. I cradle Jackson's weeping head to my chest. "But we all make mistakes when the thirst is too strong."

Jackson's mother whimpers and reaches out to her son. She hopes he will come back to her. Instead, I draw him close to me in the crevice of my high-octane arms. My superior body reminds him that he is not defined by weakness.

I press another bottle of Muscle Water to Jackson's lips and he slurps it up between bellyaching hiccups and a stream of tears. I console him, running my fingers through his hair, stopping only to break up the day-old, gel-caked knots.

"Don't cry, wild boy," I say. "You can still be a man. Believe in your thirst. Believe in me."

THE MOTEL CALIFORNIA

AMANDA CECELIA LANG

IT'S LATE WHEN I arrive at the soul-trap this town calls the Motel California. Lightning ignites the snowy sky, and the volunteer ambulance is already making its quiet exit.

"County medical examiner," I tell the deputy outside the commune's massive steel gates. He waves me through, and my headlights crisscross the weedy snow-globe acres, joining red-flashing police lights and barely controlled chaos. Smalls towns aren't equipped for this. Beyond the motel's sagging walls, random state troopers have corralled twenty-odd men and women festooned in stage sequins and rock-n-roll leather. I could hear their eerie neon chants back at the gates. Now, parking my meat wagon beside two highway cruisers and the sheriff's SUV, I can decipher loose off-key lyrics.

"*...radio static, cosmic voice...midnight signals from the void...*"

That old song. Brings back memories I don't want, not tonight.

I kill the engine. Barely have my seatbelt free when Thomas Atkins yanks my door open—white cowboy hat, harried eyes, once known in certain circles as the dope king of Sagebrush High. These days, for better or worse, he's Sheriff Thom. "Christ, Joan, what took you so long? We've got a real shit show here."

I almost tell him he's lucky I came at all, but grab my field kit instead. Like there's anyone else to do this, not in a hundred cornhusk miles. I slide out into the storm, and Sheriff Thom appraises my wrinkled scrubs and red-stinging eyes, maybe for schisms.

"Sure you're up for this? She ain't pretty, Joan."

"High school was twenty years ago," I say without much choice. "Ali and I are dust."

"They call her Mother Star now." But he clears his throat, swallows back the old joke. Turns out, despite years of local punchlines, nothing's funny about this UFO ranch.

"Mother Star," I mutter, following Thom across the gravel courtyard. What's in a name, right? *MTV* called her Nova Moon all throughout her rock goddess '80s, and in the tabloid '90s, *Sixty Minutes* branded her lights-in-the-sky commune "The VIPs of Rock-N-Soul."

Smoke and mirrors, fame or infamy—she'll always be Alison Johnson to me. My one-time best friend with her Ouija board and shitty grades and too-short gym shorts, the first girl I ever kissed.

"So, what's it looking like?" I finally ask, the words sticking in my throat. "Homicide, suicide?"

"Christ, Joan, that's your call. This one turned my stomach stranger than what happened to the cattle on those ranches last fall. Got some of them claiming she ain't really dead. We're lucky the news choppers ain't circling yet. Paparazzi's gonna be on this like vultures."

He scowls at Ali's VIP disciples, those lucky elite who breezed her auditions. Glossy women and rugged men, supermodel faces, glam-rock voices. Even corralled behind police tape, they radiate unearthly Hollywood charisma, flaunting zip-tie restraints like fashion statements. As we pass, they strain against the overstretched troopers, waving devil horns and singing louder in defiance of my very existence. They've no use for lower-dimension death-workers like me.

"*...dream in colors not of Earth...the mothership awaits rebirth...*"

"Real chart-topper," Thom quips. Despite his sarcasm, he's not wrong.

He steers me toward the motel's far end, Room 13, if I had to guess. Ali's old lucky number. "Already got twenty-six in custody. Don't know what the hell to call 'em. Suspects, witnesses, victims… I need manner and time of death clocked ASAP, close as you can manage, anyway. She's a damn mess, Joan."

He briefs me as we maneuver the sleet-slick walkway, ducking against the snow. At approximately 11:00 p.m. tonight, his office received an anonymous call. Someone at the Motel California was dying, but the ritual was still in motion. Thom requested backup from state troopers, then wrangled two deputies and burned rubber out here. A decade of rumors about UFO seances and interstellar radio rituals hadn't prepared them for what they'd find.

The door to Room 13 hangs open, guarded by yellow police tape. Snow flurries pepper the red-carpet threshold, and oil lanterns cast fluttery burnt-amber light around the room's perimeter. A wavering human shadow reclines on the bed.

I hesitate outside the door and take a deep breath, fishing my kit for PPE. "No electricity?"

"Never paid their energy bill."

"They went without heat?"

"Went without lots. First thing being common sense. Whole cult was just milling around her, singing and humming same as flies around roadkill. Still won't shut up."

"The music keeps her spirit tethered."

"Come again?"

"Read it in a pamphlet once." I shrug.

Thom side-eyes me while we snap on protective gloves and masks. I draw out the seconds as long as possible before I have to step inside with her.

"You ready?"

As I'll ever be. My chest is pounding, ears buzzing. Room 13 is like entering a meat locker, or another world. Snow crystals glitter the lantern-lit air, and everything feels heavier, like trudging through a dream with mirrored ceilings. For the first several steps, I follow my penlight, clocking every detail except what's on the bed.

The air reeks of marijuana, and another oily-sweet scent bleeds inside my mask. My light gleams off syringes and bongs, baggies of glittery herbs and jars of murky metallic juices. Everything will have to be bagged and tagged for tox screens in the city.

"I ordered them to drop their instruments like weapons." Thom shines his light along the floor. Rain sticks, hang drums, bow chimes. So many, I have to step over them.

On the bed, Ali's old steel string rests canted in her arms. Same guitar she used to strum in my bedroom at night—same one she played in her "Transcendent Hearts" video and posed with on the cover of *Rolling Stone*. Her record label loved selling her as the rebel farm girl who made it big. Big album sales, big stadium tours, big fan love. Her diehards mimicked her sequins and leather. They gathered in mobs outside her limos and chanted her lyrics. Her first big taste of being worshiped. Maybe she started craving it, maybe it was inevitable. Ali always did have a magic about her. A way of making me feel like we were the only souls alive. But those private moments are bygones. Ali only spoke to me a few shaky times after she skipped town for California, after the summer of '81.

That one perfect summer. The season *it* happened.

"Ever seen anything like her?" Thom says, startling me. I realize I've frozen near the bed, penlight poised on that guitar, gaze set firmly in the past.

I look up and, after all this time, Ali and I make eye contact.

My light trembles, but I hold her in the spotlight, try not to sick up my supper.

Nova Moon, Mother Star…sweet mercy, Ali, what've you become? I can't look away. She's like a relic from a museum.

Coppery leather skin vapor-locked to her skeleton, sharp cheekbones, desiccated smile, sunken eye-sockets. That slick milky gaze. She doesn't look like the dewy, strawberry-lipped girl I once loved. She doesn't look like the feral, moon-spangled rockstar who slipped between my fingers.

She doesn't look like a person.

I shudder, feel Thom squeeze my shoulder. She *looks* like the mummified extraterrestrial on the cover of her last studio album.

Right down to the prairie flowers and backstage passes decorating that naked husk. Right down to the daggers positioned around her like sunbeams. How hideously prophetic, how self-fulfilling. All she's missing are the glowing blue eyes.

"They told you she was still dying?" I half-laugh, gut-sick. Wish I never answered Thom's call tonight. Holy hell, I wish so many things. "Fuck's sake, look at her. She's been dead for weeks, maybe months."

Thom looks out of his depth. "There's something else, maybe why they kept her like this. This crazy weather, the icy cold room. Except, if you touch her… Joan, I think she's still warm. Feverish even. Almost as if…"

That's ridiculous. He's falling down their rabbit hole. Because look at her! Her pupils don't respond to my light. Ice crystals sparkle in her shaggy jet-black hair. They don't come colder or deader.

Then why am I suddenly desperate to touch her? What's this grisly spark of hope?

I kneel, stirring old shadows. It feels like crossing a barrier, like entering Ali's private bubble. Wasn't it always warmer here? I clasp her hand, and sure as hell…

She feels hot.

Her forehead, her chest, everything radiates impossible fever, even through my exam gloves. "Holy shit, Thom."

"What do you make of it?"

I shake my head. It's the lantern heat, or some homebrewed embalming tincture we'll discover in the tox screens—calcium chloride maybe, or a phosphorus compound. Something to give the skin this blushing coppery warmth. I lift Ali's hand off the guitar with a dull-steel twang, surprised by her rag-doll pliability. No rigor mortis. And no lividity, far as I can see, no bruising, no ghastly settling of blood. And where are the blowflies and their eggs? Whoever preserved her did a hell of job. I dig a tympanic thermometer from my kit, then tuck Ali's messy rebel hair behind one ear. Like old times. I'm dying to lean close, whisper, *Have you missed me?* Instead, I gentle the thermometer into her ear and wait for the beep.

101.3°F

I show Thom, my own blush rising. 101.3—same as our old favorite radio station.

101.3 FM The Zone, music that takes you there!

"That can't be normal." Thom steps back, rests an unconscious hand on his holster.

Half-expecting Ali to grab me, I press tentative fingertips against the pulse point in her wrist, tell myself there's nothing flickering below this latex-thin membrane of unreality.

Outside, strange lightning electrifies the frosty sky. The VIPs go wild, dialing up their volume, scream-singing Ali's greatest hit like they sense my blasphemous touch. I can practically feel them straining against their binds.

"Pulse is illusion, watch it hide…follow, leave the Earth behind…"

A gunshot cracks the open night.

Thom ducks behind the doorframe, then comes up scrambling, gun unholstered. Almost looks like a real sheriff, though I bet imposter syndrome sinks in fast. Ali's VIPs have always been a town nuisance, digging through dumpsters to feed their flock, selling hallucinogens, scattering flyers for their ragtag concerts and coveted auditions. But this—

I pray that was a warning shot. Outside, radio voices splinter and lose the melody, shouting lyrics while troopers bark frantic orders.

"Stay where you are, stay together!"

"…returning on the cosmic tide!"

"Hands where we can see them!"

"…lift you to the other side!"

"Down on the ground!"

"Lord help us if the news choppers swoop in and see this." Thom dips his hat out into the storm. "Stay with the body, Joan, I've gotta wrangle this shit-circus!"

He disappears into the snow and lightning, slamming the door behind him, auto-locking me inside. My very own backstage pass. Lanterns flutter, voices echo like heartbeats.

And just like that, for the first time in twenty years, Ali and I are alone together.

AS THE LONE medical examiner in a five-town territory—the outermost being my childhood home—sometimes my subjects are folks I grew up around. Church ladies, the grizzled mechanic, the carefree somebodies I saw dancing along Main Street. Heart attacks, car accidents, but when they return to me, the wounds never sting. Greeting them, finally getting to know familiar strangers, how they lived, how they died, that's the gift my life gives me. Ali always said everyone's born with a secret calling. Me, I'm the last person who sees inside the dead, the final witness to their secrets.

I secure the chain-lock on the motel room door then unpack my kit. Syringes, specimen jars, evidence bags, a disposable camera.

Strange though, uncanny really, how presenting Ali with the grim tools of my trade floats me like an out-of-body experience. I need to take fluid and tissue samples, snap some red-carpet photos. But who am I to desecrate a shrine? Look at her, a goddess anointed in glitter and backstage passes. Lamplight glistens like wishes across her sunken coppery skin.

I kneel close. "Where're you traveling, Ali? What've you seen up there?"

Lock jaw or silent treatment, she doesn't answer, not out loud—but did *I* even speak out loud? As best friends, we used to telegraph our thoughts with the twist of a smile, the glint of an eye. But the planet is loud tonight. Sounds like Sheriff Thom found himself a bullhorn. All those muffled commands, all those voices outside our window.

"*...phantom whispers, stellar sighs...broken people hear the cries...*"

I lean into Ali's sheening milky gaze. Did she tell our secrets? Definitely, she told what we saw that final summer. Strange powers that unlocked her, lights above the rooftops, the sudden prophetic dazzle of the lyrics on the radio. She wove that extra-terrestrial flare into her own lyrics, told *MTV* VJs and *Rolling Stone* reporters, teased it out to flocks of devoted fans—fans who'd later be auditioned and sifted down and love-bombed. She revealed what countless rockstars, Earth's chosen lyrical messengers, have been forever telling us. *Break on through to the other side...don't fear the reaper...I saw a shimmering light...going up to the spirit in the sky...* Truth, transformation, ascension, it's everywhere. One just has to *listen*. Ali knew that, even when we were just seventeen. But in all those interviews, all those songs, I never heard her mention the greatest miracle from our summer of '81. The truly transcendent magic.

Did she ever lean in close and tell her VIPs the only secret that matters? Two small-town girls in love, breaking all the rules, plucking heartstrings like a song that never ends.

"Did you tell them who I am, Ali?"

I prepare a syringe, find myself mirrored inside her eyes. Once the heart stops pumping—if it truly has—sometimes the best place for a blood draw is an eyeball. A small souvenir.

A sharp *ping*—my needle hits glass.

I recoil, bumping the guitar off her chest with a discordant twang. Glass marbles stare back at me—how'd I miss that? Ali's VIPs took her eyes! Not uncommon in ritualistic preservation, but they didn't stop there.

Beneath her guitar, I find an array of open chest wounds.

Thirteen little songless screams.

One for every dagger adorning her shine. I angle in deep with my penlight. Note the absence of hemorrhaging, the pale bloodless edges. These gashes were made posthumously.

Glancing toward the chained door, I slide out of my mask and gloves. Ali won't mind, raw touch always was her specialty. I probe my fingertip inside the center wound, force it through subcutaneous tissue and cartilage, into the thoracic cavity. All the way down to her feverish 101.3°F heart.

Does it flinch at my touch? A little flutter?

"*...trailing stars behind...blood and pulse rewind...*"

Voices echo from outside, or from the loop inside me, hard to tell. Lyrics move like blood in my veins. Like all those nights outside hotels, all those tour cities, cheering with the fans as Ali ducked into her limo. I know all about wounds to the heart. It's part of the ceremony, part of the show. Her VIPs are trying to reignite her, chanting the path for her mothership to return.

They've probably been poking her heart for weeks, waiting for the bleed.

But Ali wasn't ready to come home. Because home isn't this planet, isn't this crude Motel California commune.

"Who've you been waiting for?" My finger trembles inside the ultimate pulse point. I lean close enough for a kiss, close enough to smell champagne and cassia on her lips.

But still this silent treatment.

Have it your way, Ali. I pull free and stab her with my needle, sharp and deep, and draw the plunger. The heart's the other best place to find postmortem blood. Glittery crimson-black plasma bubbles into my syringe, sparkling like a tiny universe.

I press the vial against my ear, indulge its uncanny heat, and there—is that music? No song rings more intimate than death. Death tolls at the true heart of every religion, every fear, every dream. How to escape it with those we love.

Sometime we plug ceremonial daggers into old wounds, one by one, like I do now. The tips of the blades slide in smoothly, all the way to thirteen, until daggers rise from Ali's chest like celestial sunbeams. We all have our talents, our rituals.

After Ali, I never truly dated. Maladroit and mousy through-out college then med school, I was the space-cadet with the stellar grades and the Nova Moon fetish, the resident with the hippy-dippy bedside manner whose advisors steered toward death services. I'm the heartbreak who never found my chosen family. But I've met countless families on the slab. I used to believe I heard songs in their blood, like Ali heard voices in her guitar. I was wrong. The grim gaspings of strangers are blips next to Ali's spotlight magic.

Her blood in my vial radiates utopia. And I hear her, I do, echoing from afar, trailing newfound stars, fresh promises on her champagne tongue. Our first kisses were our last, and much later, I failed her auditions. Year after year, and how cruel that Nova Moon should bask in Hollywood limelight without me. How cruel that Mother Star should uproot her VIPs from California and move them to our home town—to the very motel where we first ignited.

And when VIP audition flyers papered Main Street, when I polished my same old smile and knelt outside her massive steel gates, what did she tell me?

Outside Room 13, a second gunshot explodes.

Angel-song shatters into screams and bullhorn feedback. Sheriff Thom might be losing his grip. Another gunshot ricochets, fades to heartbeats of stunned silence. *Silence-silence...*

And what did Ali tell me?

I press her blood against my lips and clench my eyes in prayer, tasting faint echoes. She made promises atop this very motel beneath a circle of spinning lights, flesh clinging to summer-hot flesh. Same subliminal promises Nova Moon hid inside her lyrics, same mantras that pulse and call to so many.

But her song was only meant for me. I hear it, I hear—

The six-chord strum of her guitar.

It electrifies the air, vibrates my pulse points. I open my eyes. Ali's dagger wounds are bleeding.

Her long-held voice exhales. *"You know what you must do..."*

"ALI?" BLOOD PULSES from thirteen stab wounds, glittering around lucky daggers. Everything about this should be impossible. Everything about love feels impossible, too, sometimes. But look at us now.

Ali's sparkle always outshined me. Some are born to be loved by millions, others to be loved just once. She said her radiance darkened my desperate shadows. I needed to find my own calling, my own light, my own dazzle in the sky.

"...never the hour, never the place...then sweet death alights your face..."

Voices call from far away, but they've lost the melody. Distant cries clash in a distant world. Gunshots glisten. Lightning crashes.

"You're ready for me, Joan," Ali whispers deep inside. I brush her guitar strings, sense the micro-pulse of strawberry lips. *"...grim is the elixir, grim is your star..."*

Ali cocks her head, waiting.

I swallow her vial of blood.

Coppery, venomous, champagne kiss. She needs me, she does. I hear her, feel her rhythms tingling.

"Joan." The voice is so loud, I startle, turning toward the locked-chain door. *"No, Joan, over here, you know where utopia hides."*

Ali's voice vibrates from the back wall. From a secret doorway, a hidden passage, old as the motel itself. A silhouette wavers inside, backlit by stars, the brightest shadow I've ever cast. Wispy, disembodied, beautifully unearthly, the face on the album cover, the face of she who sings from the sky.

"...we can shine like gods, brighter from afar..."

There is nothing to fear. We've taken this journey before, Ali and I. First time that secret passage whispered open, a breeze cooling our sweat, we'd clutched each other and giggled. How sleazy, how intriguing. What could we do but follow?

"Joan!"

Fists pound the door. Sheriff Thom, shouting. The door swings inward, catches on the chain. "Joan, open up! It's a deathwatch out here!"

I don't hesitate.

I sweep Ali into my arms, bones and skin, blades and guitar, light as snow, electric as lightning. We disappear down the passageway as the door slams open.

Strings of Christmas lights lead the way down a splintery corridor. We pass behind VIP motel rooms like shadow-box glimpses behind the scenes. Guitars, sequins, radios with universal dials. Everyone wants to be like Ali. Everyone wants to be a translator for galactic gods, to shine the way home, to lead those who listen to utopias in the sky.

But Ali in my arms sings brightest.

Her hand strums that old guitar to the rhythm of my footsteps. I am running, running toward a new light ahead. Another doorway, and stairs leading heavenward.

"Joan!" Thom hollers from somewhere distant, but I don't look back.

Ali and I were born to chase the stars.

We go up and up, until we burst into the snowy night, top of the motel, practically top of the world. We've been here before, though it looked different twenty years ago, under the lights.

Tonight, I find a landing pad for our starship.

Steel beams and catwalks reminiscent of stage rigging. I ascend a metal staircase, and the landing pad wobbles. Snow dusts Ali's glass eyes and the array of bloody steel daggers. My arms tremble under the weight of her heartbeat. In the parking lot below, sequin-and-leather bodies redden the snow while others kneel, assume the position. Atop the landing pad, I stand taller than I ever dreamed possible and hold Ali up like an offering to the universe.

Lightning awakens, branching across the snow-feathered sky.

As it fades, new lights appear, turning void into spectacle, blinking brighter, one, two, thirteen. Like that night in '81, these neon lights spin, pushing down on us with the gravity of wind and cosmos. I didn't understand then, but I do now.

I hold Ali higher, and the universe thunders open.

Lightning reaches down and grips us.

Sizzling, electric, intergalactic pyrotechnics, infinitely hotter than 101.3°F. The intensity of it flashes through Ali and into me. The current runs circular, heartbeat, melody. Daggers turn molten in her chest, lyrics fusing us together as the fabric of the universe burns apart, sequins and leather, galactic gods peering down.

Ali's eyes glow blue like her album cover.

I collapse onto my knees.

"Holy Christ, Joan!" calls a faraway voice. But not Ali. No, Ali's here in my arms, inside my ears. Above us, the spinning starship brightens, lights condensing into a glittering spotlight. Calling us to ascend. Together. Forever.

My eyes close against the brilliance, veins sizzling and blistering, heartbeat receding down a long secret corridor.

"Joan!"

When I open my eyes, smoke rising from my breath, I discover a silhouette crouching over me.

White cowboy hat, harried eyes, a man out of his depths up here. Sheriff Thom tries to prop me up, but my charred skin sluffs away. That's okay. Soon I'll be wearing sequins and leather. "Joan, *Joan*, hold on for the ambulance. Hell were you thinking?"

"She's here," I gasp, fire and smoke. "She brought the lights for us…"

The whirling radiance glistens through Ali's shaggy charcoal hair. Her hand falls limp, strums the guitar one last time.

"*…eternity is cause of death…in these arms, unending breath…*"

"Damn paparazzi," I hear Thom curse amid wind and spotlights and screeching concert feedback. And even as my breath smolders, my arms remain fused around the first girl I ever kissed, the only one who ever loved me.

My star who millions worship. All of them praying to know her and be her and be loved like her. Forever in the limelight. Lights in the sky. Our shadows taller than our souls. And as my heartbeat loses the rhythm, I don't fear. I know where I'm gonna go when I die, and the promise fills me with magic and lightning.

And Ali.

YOU MADE ME WANT TO KILL THE WORLD

CATLYN LADD

"THE FIRST TIME Jesus died to save humankind," you told me. "The second time, She will live, and it will be the world that dies on the cross."

You made me want to kill the world. You made me feel like God.

We sat on a low, stone wall passing a cigarette back and forth, watching the lights come on as the sky turned dark. The stone wall had been built on the only hill for miles, and we sat gazing over the flat. The lights glittered below, insignificant and trashy.

"To take out a town, take out the electric grid first," you said.

I turned away from the city below. Your profile against the night sky looked regal. Roman. I thought of Sekhmet, goddess of war.

"Or poison the water," I said. "Take out half the population before they know what's happening."

Your eyes were so dark. I saw myself reflected there, trapped inside your perception of me. I had forgotten how to be anyone else.

"I love your mind," you said, making me laugh. "Where would you get that much poison?"

"I wouldn't have to get it," I replied. "Hacking into the water treatment plant allows access to removed contaminants. Lye could be released into the water at levels high enough to kill, burn, blind, and otherwise incapacitate."

"And otherwise incapacitate," you repeated. "I love how you talk."

I preened under your praise. "How do I talk?"

I remember that you took my hand, your fingers curling over mine. I didn't think then that there is always a final touch: When did I touch you for the last time? That's something I should remember.

I do remember the last time I saw you. You looked back at me over your shoulder and your lips curved up in that smile just for me. It was too bright through the open door and smoke poured around your body like a special effect. A shout came through that door and you turned, the smoke obscuring what happened next. But I knew. I see it still, even though I couldn't have seen it happen. I was lying face down on the floor with a boot on my back when it happened.

"I will make a religion out of you," you told me. I didn't think it was cliché. I had never imagined anyone like you; how could you be a stereotype, your words a trope?

We were violence, you and I, two chemicals brought together for combustion. Benign on our own and deadly when combined.

They don't tell you how exciting it is, doing bad things. They tell us that only evil people commit murder, that such people must have been born wrong. "I knew there was something not right about her," the neighbor says on the news, her expression eager. But she didn't know a damn thing; smiled at me every time she saw me, offered me plates of cookies, eggs fresh from her hens, a length of yellow fabric. And she'd doted on you, the old, lying flirt.

It built gradually, our Plan, sweetly seductive. It all started so innocently, with conversations after Environmental Science, lying under the trees outside Harmon Hall, somnambulant in the shade. We'd watched *An Inconvenient Truth*, been reading environmental ethicists, and they all agreed: The world was fucked. There were too many people. I remember when you said: "The only way to save it is if about ninety percent of humans die."

"The bigots go first," I'd replied. "Bury them alive, throw them from airplanes, feed them to tigers."

You'd laughed and kissed my temple. My violence turned you on.

I closed my eyes against the sunlight, imagining how quiet it would be when the traffic fell silent, when the planes dropped from the sky, when the heady human hum died away. You made me realize that the only way to spend every moment with you was if the rest of everything ceased to exist.

"We have been foretold," you said, and I smiled in the warmth. We felt destined, born with purpose. "We were born to save this world."

The last time I touched you had to be that terrible day. We awoke together, curled in bed. We had coffee; I remember how my fingers grazed yours when you handed me the mug. In the car you would have laid your hand on my thigh the way you always did. Was that the last time? I don't remember if later we touched when I passed you the gun.

You plan and plan so that everything goes perfectly, but it never does. I don't know what tipped off the guard sitting bored at the information desk, but she raised the alarm and that's when everything started to go sideways. A siren brayed and the security doors began to trundle down.

I slid a rolling chair under each side of the metal grate descending from the ceiling. The chairs creaked and bent but stopped the door. You slipped underneath. I handed you the gun.

"Keep the escape route open," you told me.

I moved another chair into place, just to be safe. Inside the lab, I heard glass break.

Our contingency plan consisted of bombs and bolt cutters. It worked pretty well, but you refused to give up on the main objective: the Anthrax stored inside the lab. I screamed at you to let it go, to hurry, but you disappeared into the bright smoke.

Our plan wasn't a new one: it's been tried before. Charles Manson murdered people to start a race war between the police and Black people. The Japanese cult Aum Shinrikyo bombed the Tokyo subway, trying to make it look like the Russians did it to start World War III. We figured we could do the plan better.

After that Environmental Sciences class, I signed up for

programming and you took the biochemistry route. Our apartment filled with books and computers. And friends. Devotees.

Prophets always have disciples. Ours found us. Chance took an advanced chemistry class with you and the two of you bonded over bong hits and Donkey Kong. Brenda taught me how to hack and we started challenging each other: the city council, the transportation system of New York City, the country of Kyrgyzstan. Stephanie started studying explosives and Wayne took on building us a place to be when the world destructed. Brenda and I moved over a million dollars into an offshore account, taking just a few dollars from thousands of individuals. By the time we graduated, we had a plan. And guns. And bombs. And fake identities. Everything doomsday prophets needed.

That day, everything went perfectly. At first. Brenda and I accessed the municipal water plant with no difficulty. We had practiced several times, just getting in but not doing anything. On that day we purged the toxic waste back into the town's drinking water. Pandemonium ensued. We set up lawn chairs on the roof of the short-term rental we were staying in and watched the emergency vehicles. You streamed the news on your tablet. Body bags started appearing on the sidewalks. The small ones bugged me a little. But not too much. It was the price, and it was worth paying.

They called it a terrorist attack and started looking for brown suspects. Six white, beer-drinking, twenty-somethings watching the chaos from a roof didn't strike anyone as suspicious. A cop even wandered by and told us to keep drinking from cans. Avoid the water. Don't take showers. You called down a thank you and she tipped you a jaunty salute.

We waited until four that afternoon, an hour before closing time, and walked in like we owned the place. We had forged credentials, thanks to Brenda. And the mag strips on them really worked, showing us to be lab techs from the CDC. We signed in no problem, you flirted with the security guard, making her blush. It should have gone according to plan, but she must have heard something. Maybe when I used the bolt cutters on that cabinet door? My ID card was supposed to work as a key card, but it didn't. Forcing the blades between the metal jamb of the door made a little noise but not that much. It shouldn't have been enough for her to hear.

I had almost all the little vials out of the cabinet when the alarm went off. Those innocuous little jars all clinking together companionably ready to unleash death. Marburg, Ebola, Francisella Tularensis; such sweet little viruses all ready to go airborne, breathed into soft-tissue lungs.

But the big money was Anthrax. One gram can kill over a million people. Releasing it into the airports across the Americas and Europe was stage one of our plan to end humanity's dominion over the earth. And it has a convenient vaccine, which we also planned to swipe.

We dreamed of quiet trees regrowing in the rainforest, pollution in the oceans deteriorating, reincorporating into the waters. We fantasized about vines pulling down skyscrapers, garbage dumps disappearing beneath moss and mushrooms. Original sin was doing nothing. We would make the world anew, you and I, a new primordial couple. Bigotry washed down the drain, weapons rusting in their concrete cages, the select few repopulating with love and wisdom as the central premises. Our babies would be born golden and perfect, racism washed away.

The bray of the alarm startled me so badly that I almost dropped the bag. I knew all the vials were shatterproof, but it still gave me a turn when they clattered together. I took a deep breath and zipped the bag.

"Okay, no problem," I whispered and walked to the door. Looking quickly up and down the hall, I saw no one. I let myself out and walked purposefully toward the exit, obeying the alarm.

Behind me, a door closed softly and I glanced over my shoulder. You shot me a nervous smile. The bag in your hand hung limply. You had gone in search of the Anthrax.

It all happened so fast then. I saw the emergency grates trundling down over the door. I shoved a chair underneath, and it creaked under the weight. You ran past me, taking the gun, and said, "One more lab. Hold the door."

I called after you, but you didn't hear me. Glass broke.

I didn't hear the officer come up behind me. The siren was too loud. I wasn't expecting them; they should have all been occupied with the chaos we'd caused outside. When he slammed me into the ground, my front tooth chipped on the linoleum and the breath went out of me. I dropped the bag and hoped one of those vials would defy physics and break.

You appeared in the doorway on the other side of the grate. A flash strobed around you, lighting up your curls like a halo. Smoke poured down the hall. You turned, your hands coming up. You glanced back at me. That smile. The cop shoved me down. I heard the AK fire.

Now I sit in my prison cell, eyes closed, and dream of you. I see you in sunlight, the dusting of freckles along your cheekbones. Your turn to me with that smile, and all I can think is that prophecies are a lie. You died choking on white phosphorus, and you didn't rise from the dead.

THUMB SUCKER

L. P. RING

THE COMMUNITY, THE job—the "out there." The house, the marriage—the "in here."

Out there, sympathy fatigue has curdled to impatience, to eyerolls, or sighs. To gossip—what else is there to talk about except scripture, children, and other people? To avoidance. Alex is a jinx, a hex. A reminder of life's fragility. A warning against non-belief. All her fault.

In here, in this mood-sensitive prison which they could only ever sell to fellow Brethren, it's Alex's fault too. Where without work she'd exist as red eyes and hangovers. Her fault. Where she sits with eyes glazing over as she's typing out school reports or as the VT Screen flashes cookery shows, news, and weather. Where she lies wide-eyed in the dark, her treacherous mind flashing images of lost happiness. All her fault.

"Did you suck your thumb as a child?" Max's voice jolts her back to reality.

Biscuit shifts at her feet, doggy ribs rubbing like book spines across the tips of her toes. Questions about childcare and development—mental, emotional, or physical—are increasingly their only interaction. Max has made clear his unwillingness to "walk on eggshells" any longer.

Not all kids are our kid, Alex.

"Your mother might have weaned you off your thumb with a pacifier," he continues, eyes judging her almost blank work screen. The embryologist savant is mining for another childhood foible. A cute anecdote will preface a scavenger hunt through hard drives for her childhood photos: baby pics, kindergartens, family trips. He never looks to his own family's albums. His family wouldn't allow *that*.

"Why the interest?" Alex asks.

Max is leaning against the door jamb, the heat from his body switching the mood-respondent wall between cherry and cerise. "It's cute."

"What's cute about him not needing Mommy to have a good time?" His. Him. He? Who made this imaginary, appendage-sucking brat a him? One made of toads and snails and puppy dog's tails.

"It's an expression of independence—the child taking his first steps towards self-actualization." There's a pregnant pause as Max seems to mentally note another presentation point.

From there right up to borrowing the car without asking. If that happened, the parents—like Alex's mom, for example—could just stick the kid in boarding school. If that didn't take, they could move to a religious community that honors amputation to ascertain and advertise faith.

Alex is gritting her teeth. Max crouches and clicks his middle finger and thumb twice. Biscuit burrows further back. The wall behind Max shimmers between charcoal gray and mauve. Mood-respondent wall settings always predict incoming squalls. She turns back to the blinking cursor, which displays the sentence, "Charlie has worked really hard this year." That little shit has not.

"No conference slides of me, right?" Alex asks. The mere memory of that last presentation he used her picture for makes her squirm.

"That was only to show off my loving relationship," Max says, but doesn't say the part about his wife keeping all her fingers and toes, clothed modestly, happy.

See, the Brethren always say, parading her or her sister Cassie around, *fulfilling all duties and sacrifices is a choice. We're not savages lopping off limbs...*

"Parents worry thumb-sucking leads to problems with the palate, the teeth, jaw alignment..." Max trails off. Like a university lecturer, he's coming to terms with the class not having done the reading.

Dylan never sucked his thumb. Never. Never. *Never.*

"Ask Mom." Alex lets out a long, low breath as his tread recedes. Mothers-in-law are the ultimate red-button deterrent.

Max makes a peevish comment about ordering take-out again before his office door slams. The walls settle on storm-cloud gray. Alex runs her tongue over her gumline, inside and out. Forward and back along her mouth's roof from soft palate to hard ridge. No misshapen clefts. No misalignments.

Melanie, Alex's coworker, has a spoiled brat who is Dylan's age now. Alex pictures a bright red balloon tethered to Melanie's eldest's pudgy right thumb. She imagines the string snapping, the boy's blubbering before he might seek the solace of *his* thumb…

She thinks of Dylan now, and the walls turn to a burnished umber. A pinch of jealousy is surely forgivable.

So is lying to the terminally ill.

A kindness like reading bedtime stories, promising the nurse would come or the doctor would fix the pain. It hurts, it hurts, it all huuuuuurrrrttts. The pain killers, which stopped working. The disinfectants mingling with that other smell. As the programmed clinic walls and ceilings showed collages of animals and animation characters with saffron and vermilion, fuchsia and lavender, which Max loved and insisted they install in their home to "keep Dylan calm."

Because the body does not fail if one's faith is real. Isn't this why true Brethren pare back the whole? To strengthen the core? To show faith in His word? This is why…

The cursor blinks, blinks, blinks. "Close file. No, save," she says with a sigh.

She hovers at Max's door. He'll be nuancing his sales pitch for all the birthing agencies, dropping buzz words, promising the world. Maxwell Donald Watson has his metaphorical finger on the pulse of the collective buying public. The gift. The patter. No citing surveys, discussing palate strength or gum measurement for this wunderkind. Investors barely listen to details.

Something poking at Alex's calf almost makes her cry out. Biscuit's finally out from beneath the table, her tail wagging slightly as she looks up inquiringly. She's Team Alex. Not impatient, not bored. Alex treads to the front room; Biscuit's nails tap on the flooring as she follows. Biscuit—that name was Dylan's choice.

Max's latest idea keeps gnawing at her as she pours the Chardonnay. She remembers that awful engagement dinner. That hurried shush and awkward silence when Cassie's fiancé dropped *that* term: "Menu babies." Alex caught people's pained expressions, pursed lips, and eyerolls while Max got rolling with the usual corrections. Those strident justifications: the honor of perfected procreation, social contracts, better living through technology, blah-blah-blah. Don't let anyone ever tell you there can't be disagreements within a cult.

"Science doesn't legislate or harm. Science is His creation in conversation with our World. Who wants to be like those Luddite "birthers" out there waddling around for nine months with their bulging bellies?" He laughed in mock disbelief.

LOLOL, indeed, Alex thinks while draining her Chardonnay. She had caught Cassie's eye then, but was too worried Max would spot a sympathetic smile. Alex stares at her hands. The Brethren mandate that thumbs are the last digits removed. Only at retirement, once an adherent has worked, contributed, and sacrificed everything. It's the others' turn to wait on them now.

Max even suggested she switch jobs. Get away from those other kids.

The digital screens along the mantel parade showcase work successes, vacations, and most importantly, a family of three in different poses. Dylan's full-featured, cherubic face, blue eyes, blonde hair, a trace of baby fat. Smiles, often gap-toothed, but no thumbs in incriminating positions. Dylan will be safe from Max's slides. No need for a heart-rending account of how naturally conceived births can fail.

The screens that replaced the bay windows offer a vista of rolling meadows. Max is all about pastoral settings these days. Alex switches it off and judges the limp, faded misery of her muted reflection steeped in Chardonnay. Without the window and wall installations Max wanted, the view would stretch for miles, past the electronic gates and compound edges towards the distant mountains, to where known becomes unknown. But of course, fake meadows rolling for hours and hours is what every woman should want to see.

The office door clicks open. Max's bare soles stick against the timber flooring, no click-click from the toe prosthetics he removes as easily as his loafers the moment he's in the door. He presses his mouth against Alex's shoulder; it takes every ounce of willpower not to shrug him off. The left index finger traces along the edge of the frame, which turns from russet to burnt umber. Max's pinkie and ring fingers were removed last year. Some say the nubs still tingle.

"It was just a glitch, Alex," he whispers, leaning into her. "We could get another."

Her mind locks at *getting* another. He squeezes both her shoulders, but of course the left one just seems more like pinching.

"Did he share your grief, Alex?" Cassie once asked.

Was his approach to the loss more clinical? Was his approach that of a father or a design savant and embryologist? Is there a difference between how a woman relates to a "bun from her own oven" and one harvested and brought to the edge of trimester three in a lab? That's what they discuss in church, right? Strive to create perfection but also embrace the wholesomeness of some trimming after the fact. This is why… This is why…

"Dylan wasn't a glitch," Alex manages, the last word almost catching in her throat.

"Sorry," Max mumbles. "Stupid work-speak."

A finger parts her hair and runs along the rough cartilage of her right ear, her sole sacrifice thus far. According to Mom, thanks to Alex's long, thick hair, it doesn't really even count as a sacrifice.

The dark reflection in the window of wife and husband, once mother and father, once anointed to be wed, and in the beginning just commune friends, stares back. Alex's eyes wander to the mantel and, as if by magic, a picture of them taken not long after she arrived is one of the portraits. She wonders at the bland yellow t-shirt she wore that summer's day—surely she couldn't have become that boring and lame so quickly. She squints, tries to remember that afternoon, but what she remembers from the "courtship" won't be any more reliable than those pictures, hued in post-tearaway guilt, with new surroundings, and spun until she was dizzy by that communal love-bombing. Then the wedding. Then Dylan. A picture smiles up at her from the mantel. Dylan wasn't a glitch. And Dylan didn't come from a Petri dish.

"I know things haven't been great lately," Max whispers, using his "sounding hurt" tone. "But I've done my best. I've worked. I've stood by you."

It's a relief when he steps away, leaving Alex alone in the window's reflection. The flooring shivers against her bare soles. When was the last time she felt carpet between her toes? A plaintive Biscuit weakly wags her tail.

Stood by you? Definitely your fault, Alex.

The body cannot survive alone. Growth and age bring weakness, require assistance from the community. She remembers Mom's retirement party. They amputated up as far as her right wrist, with Alex's stepfather's smile shining brighter with each sweep of the Gigli saw as everyone cheered. Such a commitment to the precepts of the community, to sacrifice all semblance of autonomy. Such an example. This is why the Brethren enact these lessons. Sacrifice as an act of faith in the whole. The blessed knife. The cuts to show adherence within a vessel sculpted as instructed from *His* book. This is why. Technology brings knowledge and comfort, empowers and enhances the mind and the soul. Technology creates, but still fumbles on the preservation bit.

It wasn't yellow, that t-shirt, she remembers, but machine-washed to a dull gray with Uma Thurman lying on a bed, just like in the retro-style movie poster. Certainly not suitable teenager-wear for a future elementary school teacher, wife, and mother. She wonders where that top went. She definitely can't still have it.

"Alex, honey?" Max calls from his office. He's switched to that half-coaxing, sing-song tone he uses for sex. Ignoring him isn't an option. Suffer it. Listen. Nod. Soon it'll be bedtime and she can lie still in the dark, the sheets cradling her in a velveteen shimmer while he snores beside her.

The queasiness starts from the very first image: cell-stage development, the amniotic sac, the developing embryo and fetus. The fetus. Worry turns to cold, formica-molded panic.

Get another.

A glitch.

"This time you'll leave work," Max says as his eyes slip down her left arm. "You've needed a full set of digits for working with those children. But a mother accepts help. Accepts her need through public commitment."

She shakes her head more and more vehemently. His tone turns irritated, didactic. Alex wrenches away, wincing at the bruise above her elbow. Two years of growing impatience and now this. A hypodermic of adrenaline wielded by the clenched fist of John Travolta couldn't jolt this relationship flatline.

"And when did you stop adding your cycle to the app?!" he yells after her. "Not like your moods don't say plenty!"

The walls undulate between crimson and scarlet. The woman in the reflection has had a shock. She needs to get out. Go to Mom's, Alex thinks before considering the shock with which her stepfather would greet her arrival.

Cassie's place, then. It's scary, but a map forward without Max unfurls. Visit a lawyer; to hell with what any of the community thinks. She imagines the elders trooping in, insisting she's overreacting. Insisting a great husband like Max can only mean well; he's a guide who must know best. Things will be different his way. Better.

"Shut up that mutt's growling." Max enters, flicking open a screen on his handheld pad. She's cradling her wine glass. She imagines flinging it at his head, and the walls undulate between blood red and black.

"You want CliffsNotes, Alex? You're my wife and I love you. I've looked deep into my heart, I've prayed, and am truly convinced this is the way to be a family." The words sound honeyed. "There's a mark for the thumbprint at the bottom of each page. Sign at the end." He places the device on the coffee table. "You'll put in your notice tomorrow. Phonics and the times tables bring in barely enough for vet's bills. Dealing with other people's kids. All that pointless paperwork. And your just being there upsets some of the mothers. I'm doing you a favor."

"Fuck you."

The clink of glass on bottle is paired with a sigh as he pours his wine as if he'll let the vulgar, outsider language slide for now. Max switches the screen on to his meadow view. The knee-high grass and dots of soft rush sway in a light breeze. She doesn't know how long she stares at the final page. Finally, she tosses the device aside, half-afraid it'll bite.

"Parenting and matrimony aren't prisons." Max's voice is evenly paced, but the tensity of his shoulders, the clench of his jaw all match the swirls of red across the walls. "They are gifts from Him to His chosen flock." She wants to answer that if those are only gifted to His chosen, then God must have cast His love over the unbelievers this century as well. But Max doesn't like blasphemy.

Alex thinks beyond the screen, past the perimeter fencing and commune gates. Out there might be Sodom and Gomorrah, a Hieronymus Bosch painting. Might be like one of those Clive Barker novels she read in her tearaway years before she borrowed the car keys without asking. But it would be freedom.

He pours some wine into her glass. "To us," he says as the walls shimmer blood red, a color even someone as deep in self-regard as him should see as a warning. "To new beginnings."

Her glass crunches against his right temple. He drops, roaring to his knees. Biscuit, barking furiously, leaps for him, her teeth sinking into the half-hand that grasps for Alex.

Max catches the dog by the scruff, brings his left fist down on her skull. "Get off his dog," Alex roars.

A picture from the mantel is the implement of this coup de grâce. The glass splinters from the blow; Dylan is still smiling within the flickering frame. She pulls one of the loose shards free, ignoring the slice of pain along her palm, and jabs it past Max's grasp. It pierces the iris's membrane with a dull pop, a slither of blooded puss leaking down his cheek. He tilts sideways, like a tree dropping in time to the roar of some triumphant *Timber!* call. She pulls Biscuit to her. Buries her face into Dylan's dog's neck. *Breathe. Breathe.*

Time to pack. Time to go. Stand up. There are streaks of blood on Biscuit's coat that will need washing away. No way she can go to Mom's or Cassie's now. She turns back to the window and switches off Max's meadow scene. Out beyond the dark she'll go, and whether it'll be Bosch, Barker, or Revelations, there will be something. Yes, though maybe not for Alexandra Watson. Wife, teacher, and Brethren apostate be gone.

"I bet you sucked your thumb, you self-aggrandizing shit."

She thinks of the elevator, the exits, the car. Her thumbprints won't activate any of those after dark. But there is that sharp cleaver in the drawer. The walls undulate from umber to marigold, Dylan's favorite color, she remembers. There'll be some mess due to Max's final amputation. The one suitcase will do. She'll blend in with a full set of fingers, toes, and other appendages. Biscuit nudges her calf. Alex sees hope.

THE PRICE OF FAME

NICK KOLAKOWSKI

1.

THE NAKED PSYCHO on the lawn waves a lit traffic flare and screams for God to come out and play. My first impulse is to find my phone and call the police like a good little citizen, but because this is Portland, it would take them forever to arrive, even at a bougie enclave like mine. Besides, ever since the cops stopped asking for autographs whenever they pull me over, I've liked them less and less.

As I squint through my kitchen window, I lock onto the fresh tattoo on the psycho's chest, flickering in the flare's bloody light. It's a hungover Cupid puffing on a cigarette, his wings drooping, just like I'd sketched on a paper napkin back when I first started my band. Then my gaze drifts to the scar on the psycho's neck; it's a mirror image of the one curling from my jaw down to the collarbone, only his is fresh and red instead of old and pale like mine.

I've been numb so long I can't remember the last time I reacted to anything, except for the occasional chuckle to blend in. But the sight of that tattoo and scar makes something in my mind shift and break.

"I'll take it," I say, my vision watery with tears. "It sucks, but I'll take it."

Back when journalists still cared about my opinions, they would ask how I felt about fame, to which I always replied: I have nothing but love for the fans.

Back when I still had fans, that is.

I think the last time I had a creep on the lawn, Bush II was still in office.

In the basement closet, I find my pump-action next to the Grammy for Song of the Year and a paper bag filled with 12-gauge shells. I march outside, the night air cool on my freshly shaven head, firearm held at hip level as I approach the howling degenerate. Up close, he's maybe twenty-one or twenty-two, and I almost pause as I remember myself at that age, scared shitless and chain-smoking as I waited for the Billboard charts to come out. Then the moment passes.

I aim for the tattoo on his sternum, rack the shotgun's slide, and smile.

His eyes snap open as he undertakes a split-second reevaluation of life, the universe, and everything.

I pull the trigger on an empty chamber.

Click.

If the gun were loaded, I bet that'd get people to pay attention to me again.

The psycho's mouth drops into a wide O. His left leg shakes. He tosses the sizzling, smoking flare onto the manicured grass and runs toward the gate at the driveway entrance, which he scrambles over like a spastic spider.

That's weird. I thought he'd smile or laugh back.

I need to remember all of us lunatics aren't on the same wavelength.

I return to the house, the shotgun dangling from my hand like a battle-axe in the grip of a tired Viking. My blood sings falsetto in my ears, a dull burn deep in my chest.

"Loser," I say. Whether I'm referring to the psycho or myself is an open question.

Inside, I smoke two bowls of premium weed to unkink my mind and float off to the living room, where I sink into a couch upholstered with the buttery hide of whatever exotic animal died for my relaxation. On the television, a cartoon coyote runs off a cliff into empty space and falls, keeps falling, and I find myself laughing hysterically at his predicament, which is also mine.

2.

"JIMMY, IT'S YOUR manager. Prepare to die."

Gillian's voicemail blaring from my phone's speaker, operatic with righteous fury, doesn't budge me from the couch, where I sit strumming a Stratocaster lacquered the blue of a perfect sky. Yellow afternoon light flows through the windows, prickling my skin. I have not slept in thirty-six hours, maybe more. I've been playing the same idiot chord over and over again, hoping somehow it will grow the wings of a song.

"Will you pick up already?" Recorded-Gillian says, then a pause, during which I hear her heavy breathing, almost drowned out by the testosterone roar of her lovingly restored Shelby GT500, its sound system pounding that pop she says I should start writing if I want a "comeback," as if I'd stoop to such lows.

She sucks down more oxygen and, renewed, yells: "I'm coming over, you huge jerk. I got the cops off your back for now, but at some point they're gonna want to take a statement, you hear?"

"Oh no," I tell the phone. "Scary."

"I swear, you're so returning to rehab," she mutters as the voicemail ends.

I assume this was about the psycho who called the cops. How's that for irony? Still, I don't understand what Gillian's so angry about. Her job is cleaning up messes, and a part of her berserker personality thrives on it. A long time ago, when we were kids, she used to say she had Genghis Khan blood from her mother's side. She should be thanking me for today's opportunity.

I keep playing, slipping away into that space between the notes. My hands are the ones speaking now, bones and tendons knotting and straining in symphony with the metal and string and wood. My dad had hands like these, pitted and functional as his favorite tools. When we ran errands on Saturday mornings, he would keep those hands at precisely ten and two on the wheel of the truck, taking one away only to pop the tab on the can of beer squeezed between his thighs, or cuff me on the back of the neck whenever he told a joke.

My melody begins breathing on its own. There's no better feeling than when the music is flowing through you, as if you've become the conduit for a better universe of sound and light. I'm so absorbed in my finger-work that I barely hear the front door open, a pair of heels clicking their way down the front hall to the living room.

I look up at my wife Kiera in the doorway, her crimson hair yanked into a rough bun, a grease-spotted bag in her left hand. I stop playing.

"Photographers on the street. From the news, looks like," she says, plopping down in the butterfly chair opposite me and opening the bag. She places one, two, three cartons of Chinese food on the glass coffee table between us.

"Think it'll sell albums?" I ask, knowing it won't. It's not big enough news.

She lets the silence grow electric as she peels the wrapper from a pair of chopsticks. On our first date, we went out for Chinese food and a Jet Li double-bill at the Music Box in Chicago. I hope she still thinks fondly about those days. Sometimes I want to ask if she regrets marrying me, except I'm terrified of the answer.

"Like I told you last night," she says as she pries a dumpling from a carton, "pointing guns at people isn't funny."

"I was just trying to give him a memorable experience. Autographs are so 20th century."

Kiera downs the dumpling, sets the carton on the table, adjusts the bra strap drifting down her shoulder, and gets ready to say whatever's been making her forehead crease since she came in. Sometimes people forget how well I can read them, that I'm more than a stoned Buddha. "Look," she says.

I strum a note. "Nothing good ever starts with 'look.'"

"The mortgage…"

"Damn streaming. You can have a million people listening to your songs, and you know what you get?" I hit another note. "A buck fifty. Not that I have a million people listening."

"I heard they offered Eddie and the guys two million dollars for that festival gig. One night only. You could get that." Her voice rises. "You were just as big."

"'Were' is doing a lot of heavy lifting in that sentence." I make a sound like a game-show buzzer and shake my head. "I'm a *Jeopardy!* answer, babe."

But I'm feeling good thinking about the psycho: Someone still loves my music enough to *carve a scar* on their face. How crazy is that?

She balls up her paper napkin, heavy with sauce, and throws it at my head. It hits the Stratocaster and bounces off, leaving a splatter on the shiny blue. She follows up with an icy glare before saying, in a tone of slow and infinite patience, "We need the money. Like, *really* need it. And I don't care if you have to sacrifice a goat in the middle of…"

As she speaks, I set the guitar on the couch with exaggerated care. Out of the corner of my eye, I spot a small black spider inching its way across the glass desert of the coffee table, its destination the tower of oversized photo books at the center. I let loose a banshee scream and bring my fist down on the little bastard.

When I look up, Kiera is frozen ramrod-straight, eyes so wide I can see the whites all the way around, hands balled against her chest.

"I hate spiders," I offer helpfully.

I lift my fist and the spider scurries out from underneath, untouched, harbored in the grotto between my curled fingers. I let it live a second time. Anyway, the spindly beastie is probably the reincarnation of my grandmother and crushing it will doom me to a thousand lifetimes as an even lower creature, such as a music critic.

"I'm going out," I say. "Tell Gillian 'hi' from me."

This place is starting to feel too much like a tomb.

3.

AFTER KIERA FLEES upstairs, I throw on a reasonably clean pair of sweatpants and head for the great outdoors. The news photographers aren't subtle: Two of them sit in a car parked across the street, telescopic lenses resting on their windowsills, clicking away. I put on a show for them. I stamp around, play air guitar. I give the world the finger as I march down the block and take the corner. I feel invigorated, pulsing with life.

I pull out my phone, flick to my News app, and type in my name. The first story that pops up is from a local blog with the twee name of the Vegan Vindicator: an interview with one Dwayne Matthews, my psycho gate-jumper. Dwayne looks scared as he tells heroic blogger VV, a bearded dude wearing a huge pair of elk antlers, about his weird encounter with me, his hero. "Like, I've always worshipped the guy," he babbles. "But the gun thing was seriously, seriously uncool, bro."

"Well, the guy hasn't had a hit since Y2K," VV chortles back. "And he sold his soul for cheap long before that. I wouldn't feel too bad, man."

"Oh, he had epic bangers, especially with Nightbreed. Nobody's ever had a better run, he's transcendent," Dwayne insists. "I'm covering a few of his songs tonight at Drag Queens and Doom if anyone wants to swing—"

I swipe the app closed. Sold my soul before Y2K? No, it was after that, probably sometime around '04, when I let Gillian talk me into releasing that insane double album with James Hetfield.

I realize I'm getting a little obsessed with young Dwayne.

I want to know why he loves my music.

I want to know more about that scar on his face.

There's a history of gods becoming preoccupied with their subjects. On our first album, we had a song titled "Channeling Zeus on Channel 3," which was mostly about my failure to find a girl who loved Camus like I did. Think of Zeus coming down as a swan to bang Leda. Not that I want to get romantic with Dwayne, but if he's appearing at a club tonight—why not show up?

I haven't ventured downtown in a long time, maybe years, and in the interim it has frayed around the edges. On the corner of Park and Burnside, a homeless guy stands on the hood of a stalled car, smashing out the windshield with a traffic sign.

On the sidewalks, workers on their late-afternoon commute stare at phones, doing their best to ignore the flying glass and screaming. I used to love this sort of chaos, but I don't have the knees for it anymore.

My handy phone tells me that Drag Queens and Doom is around the corner from Powell's and its amazing empire of books. I work my way in that direction, pausing every so often to gawk at a random curiosity or travesty. Everything is so loud and colorful. Everything stinks of exhaust and shit. After a few blocks, I glance behind me and realize the photographers weren't content to sit in front of my house: Two cars keep pace a half-block back, telephoto lenses and phones poking from their open windows.

I'm so flustered I almost collide with a skeletal woman in a black lace dress who's maneuvered in front of me, her gaze wild.

"Yo," she says, stepping to block my path as I try to move around her.

I look down at the bright orange box cutter clutched in her left hand.

"Greetings," I say. "I can't help you."

Her face twitches. "What?"

"I can't help anyone," I say, noting another space alien watching us from a few feet away, an older guy with a matted gray beard and sun-bleached jacket. If this is a mugging, he's backup.

"You can help by giving us some money," the lady helpfully suggests. "Or I'll cut you."

In my peripheral vision, the photographers' cars slide to a stop, ready to capture my death in high-def. I feel oddly calm, like I've already been gutted on the sidewalk and I'm watching the replay.

"When I was your age," I say, "my biggest fantasy was becoming part of the 27 Club."

The box cutter wavers. "What?" she asks.

"You know, Hendrix, Cobain, Joplin, Brian Jones. I guess Amy Winehouse is in there, too, now. But I didn't want to OD. I mean, I dallied a bit with heroin because it was expected, and I wrote a bunch of lyrics about drugs because that's what the kids wanted, but I was never really a *drugs guy*, you know what I mean?" I turn and wink at her partner.

"What the hell are you talking about?" the guy says and hitches forward, his sooty hands clenching into fists.

"So, I wanted to be a member of this great club, but I wanted a heroic death. A real samurai ending, whatever that meant. I didn't know what it actually looked like. It never happened. It was just concert after concert, album after album, year after year." I'm punching the air to my own rhythm. "Until the music industry decided I was too old. And sure, I got money and some awards and a nice house, which is a hell of a better exit package than most of my peers—"

"The money!" the lady snaps, the box cutter rising, its blade edging out.

"But a musician without an audience, it's a living death. Like being a zombie." I laugh without joy and reach forward and slap my hands on her shoulders. The box cutter tumbles from her fingers and she jerks back, startled, but my grip is too strong after so many decades of playing the guitar. "A zombie, you understand? Braaaaaaaaaains."

The guy takes his lady by the elbow and yanks her away, down the sidewalk. "Dave Grohl going nuts over here!" he yells. "I hate this town!"

I don't look anything like Dave, I want to shout back. I was never the voice of a generation. I sold a bunch of albums because, for a few wonderful years in there, a bunch of studio executives decided that everyone wanted a safe sip of darkness. And if you had a messy sound and could pair it with lyrics about losing faith and getting high, they would shower you with money until your life was ruined.

"Loser," I say, but the couple has already disappeared into the stunned crowd. I keep walking. The light is dying slowly in the eastern sky and I have a concert to attend. The photographers resume their slow roll, a few other folks also drifting in my wake—the lost, the insane, the terminally bored.

4.

PEOPLE WANT TO be followers. How else to explain the thick cluster of people streaming behind me when I finally arrive in front of Drag Queens and Doom? Precious few of them know who I am, but there's a natural urge to join a crowd. A helicopter buzzes overhead, likely the cops trying to monitor evening traffic, and yet I wouldn't be surprised if a local news crew is hunting me from the air.

Drag Queens and Doom has a nondescript front, just a glass poster-box bolted to the brick beside a black door with the venue's name in pink script along the top. By the curb, there's a metal bench where a lucky few can sit and smoke while waiting for the door to open before a show. When I first started out a million years ago, I played at so many spots like this, and I feel a pang of nostalgia heady enough to almost knock me to my knees. Or maybe that's just hunger—when was the last time I actually ate anything?

The crowd presses close. Dozens of faces—young faces—more curious than eager. I step onto the bench and see a hundred people stretching to the intersection, with more drifting our way. A forest of raised hands holding phones.

"I want to apologize," I announce.

I sense camera lenses streaming my face onto the internet, websites and Instagram and TikTok buzzing with my name. It feels like love.

"Sure, the '90s weren't great," I continue. "The LA riots. OJ. Kosovo. Waco. The Lewinsky thing. We knew it. But here's where we screwed up: We thought things were getting better. That we had the big issues solved, so long as we put in the work. We thought we had the luxury of being disaffected. That all the wars would be spiritual ones. And all that time, the rot was spreading underneath."

The crowd's energy ratchets up a few notches. I look down and see Dwayne Matthews a few feet away, his face filled with awe or maybe fear. There's a battered guitar clutched in his thin arms. He'd follow me into battle. So would the rest, but they need to know that I'm serious.

I extend a hand, and without a word, he passes the guitar to me.

The chanting begins quietly, builds quickly, until it's a roar: "*Song, song, song…*"

The guitar is a cheaper Gretsch that's seen better days, its body scuffed, the tuning pegs and fingerboard in serious need of replacement. Its weight is comforting, but another song simply won't do. The world doesn't need yet another Paranoid Android whining into the void about their feelings, even if they set it to a good beat.

The world needs someone who'll burn the rot out. Gillian was wrong: I don't need a comeback. I need a cult.

Kiera will be okay with a couple hundred people living on our lawn, right?

"So, I'm apologizing," I tell them, hefting the guitar. "My generation screwed up, just like the generation before us, just like the generation before them…"

The chanting dies out. In the rear of the crowd, someone shouts: "*You bastards!*"

"That's right," I tell that anonymous screamer, and I grin. It's like being onstage again, the energy pulsing from my soul through my fingers, the darkness crackling with fear and excitement. The crowd sucks in a collective breath and holds it, waiting.

"Look, I'm not saying I have all the answers, because when you come down to it, I'm just a guy who did some good songs before most of you were born." I'm raising my voice from deep in my lungs, loud enough to echo off the buildings around us, like a prophet straight out of the Old Testament. "But I'll always tell you the truth, because the system rejected me just like it's rejected you, and I have absolutely nothing to lose. We'll have to give stuff up, maybe even shed blood if we want to win, but—"

I trail off, realizing words alone aren't enough—they've heard a variation of this speech too many times from too many people. I feel the crowd's energy waver, like they might decide to peel away and hit up a weed shop or Powell's. These people don't need words, they need deeds.

My grip tightens on the guitar. I smile at Dwayne and he tries to smile back, the corners of his lips trembling. I don't care about his scar or his tattoo anymore, much less his reasons for loving my music, but I'll always appreciate how he renewed the fire in me.

"Hey," I tell him.

He gapes at me, expectant, hungering.

"How's God look to you now?" I say, hoisting the guitar over my head.

And with that, I leap from the bench and bring the instrument down squarely on his skull. The impact is enormous, shattering bone and wood, spraying blood on everyone within a few feet. Dwayne trembles and collapses, boneless. A good sacrifice. A good beginning.

The crowd goes berserk with glee.

DEAR DANA

SAM BRACKETT

MARCH 18TH, 2024

Dear Dana,

I got your letter. Sorry it's taken me so long to get back to you. As you can imagine, it was a lot to process, and I had to take a breather after everything you wrote. Well, actually, I "took a breather" after reading it a few times. I bet I could recite it from memory at this point, but I needed time.

I hope that you'll consider and receive every point I make as much as I considered and received each of your worries.

Let's start there, with your concern. Thank you—I really mean that.

To be concerned means you care. And to care is to love. However much we may disagree on everything else, just know that I accept your concern and recognize it for the love that it is.

At first, I didn't want to break down your concerns point by point. It felt a little bitchy and well…pointed (ha!). But I also don't know how to go about explaining why you have everything so turned upside down.

So, yes, I may end up sounding a tad defensive, but I'm at peace with that. Because the happiness that I've experienced here at Forge of Life is worth defending.

ABOUT JEREMY

I know how he must seem from the outside looking in. I read the news too, you know.

The difference between you and me, though, is that I actually read the news. Thanks to my time here, I see behind the curtain, I know what levers they're pulling and buttons they're pressing to manipulate you and so many into thinking that Jeremy is this big, spooky monster.

If I knew nothing about the amazing place that Jeremy has created here, how he's changed so many lives for the better, how he's changed my life for the better, I'd be thinking the same things as you.

But I *do* know all of those amazing things. They're the truth. And no matter how many case studies and testimonials we upload to Forge's website, those fake stories are the ones that pop up first on the search engines.

Why do you think that is? Do you have any theories?

I do.

People are scared. Everyone in the "buttoned-up world," as Jeremy likes to call it, may not know the exact methods that we've landed on out here. But here's what they do know: the power of Jeremy's results, how very real they are.

After all, the man's spent enough time with the top people of this country to know how everything works, and why they think the way they do.

Did you watch my testimonial on the website? I suspect not. So, let me break it down for you.

When I first came to Vermont, I was on all the meds they could throw at me. And I still felt crazy! I also had a couple of suicide attempts under my belt. I never told you about those, but it's true. On top of that, I couldn't stop the thoughts urging me to try again. They were unending. They formed a fog that clung to my mind, a creeping mist, soaking every last fold of my brain.

That fog began to lift the second I met Jeremy. It felt like the first time anyone actually saw me.

And then I met everyone else here at Forge and started following Jeremy's practices and, one day, I realized that oppressive haze in my skull was gone. Poof!

No more meds. No more anguish. No more pain.

In fact, it's hard for me to even recognize the person I was back then. It's like the world and everyone in my life had molded and shaped me into this sleepwalking, barely there…thing. A thing that just so happened to be living and breathing but was in no way sentient.

All it took was some honest work, a little (genuine) community, and Jeremy's guidance.

The kicker? I'm in no way the only one.

You ask anyone here at Forge and you'll see that we're all well on our way to achieving the three "Lights of Being" which are: High Peace, Eternal Love, and Magical Honesty.

Jeremy says that I've achieved two out of three already, which really is a big deal.

Think about that for a second.

No wonder the buttoned-up world is trying to kill everything that Jeremy's doing.

If Forge was able to get the word out? If Jeremy's ideas weren't actively being suppressed? Think about the effects:

Big Pharma? Done.

Psychiatry? Done.

All of that money would disappear in a flash.

And I can't even imagine what the government would do with a population of free-thinking, emotionally liberated individuals on its hands. (Hint: they'd go kicking and screaming, of course.)

So yeah, no wonder every headline about Jeremy is fear-mongering bullshit. Their livelihoods depend on it.

Let's deal with the elephant in the room. Here's what I know to be true about Jeremy: No one here has experienced anything like the accusations described in those stories. Believe me. When "the news" first broke, we had a meeting about it. Just us girls—Jeremy even encouraged it!

Not one woman in that meeting has had any interactions

with Jeremy that were inappropriate or non-consensual. Period.

Here's what I also know to be true about Jeremy (what you won't find on the news). The man is kind-hearted. He is thoughtful and considerate, honest to a fault. And, unlike everyone else, he's dedicated his life to building a better world instead of tearing it down piece by piece.

THE KIDS

I miss Albie and Ella with all of my heart. Leaving them was the hardest thing I've ever done. There are nights I cry myself to sleep thinking about them.

Can you send pictures next time? And tell me more about what they're up to? I feel like the kids I picture aren't the kids they are anymore.

I bet Albie has outgrown that train set he was so in love with. Is Ella still dancing? I bet she is. I know she is. I can see her now. Such an angel. They both are. Two little cherubs.

And yes, I can only imagine how they feel. I know how you feel, too, and I understand.

On the surface, what I've done seems selfish. In the short term, I guess it kind of is. But in the long term? I'll be the mother I was never capable of being before.

Any confusion or pain they're feeling now will be eclipsed by the Eternal Love they will receive when I'm back in their lives. When I return, I'll thank them for their sacrifice and thank you for yours. You taking care of them is the greatest gift you've ever given me.

Thank you for that, too.

Oh! And speaking of eclipses…

THE FUTURE

I know that you've wanted some sense of timeline for a while now, and I hear you. While none of the teachings or practices here at Forge of Life run by a strict schedule, I finally have an idea of when you can see me next—I can't believe it's already been three years.

As you've probably heard, the eclipse is going to pass directly over Vermont in a few weeks. Actually, I just checked my calendar, it's three weeks from today!

Jeremy has us all working overtime in preparation, and it really is going to be monumental.

If we do enough good work between now and then, Jeremy says that by the time the sun is blotted out, most (and maybe all) will achieve the three Lights of Being.

It's super exciting stuff, and I wish you could be here now to experience the energy. Everyone is buzzing.

After the eclipse, we'll all see each other again. You have my word. Until then, know that no matter what, my love for you is forever. You're my mother and nothing can ever change that.

If you take nothing else from this letter, I hope it finds you able to understand this fact and this fact alone: I'm happy and I'm at peace.

—Love, Kat

"Breaking News: Mass Casualty Event at Rural Vermont Wellness Retreat Following Eclipse"

The New York Times

Neil Fallon, April 9th, 2024

EAST BURKE, VT—Yesterday, as the moon drifted away from the sun, that rare, mid-day dawn revealed a grisly sight in the mountains of northeastern Vermont.

On the campus of Forge of Life, a controversial health and wellness center, 213 deceased were found scattered across the one-hundred-acre property.

While investigators are still gathering information and have yet to make an official statement on the matter, early indicators suggest the scene is the result of a mass-suicide event not unlike the Jonestown massacre of 1978.

East Burke police and fire departments responded to a 911 call reporting a fire in the early hours of Tuesday morning. Frank Worth, an East Burke resident, had been getting ready to leave for work when he noticed a blaze in the hills beyond his property. "When I saw the fire up there, I knew exactly where it was. Had no doubt it was that Forge of Life place," Worth told the *Times*. "Of course, who knew that's what they would find up there? I mean, everyone gave those folks their distance. They didn't have the best reputation around here. So, I can't say that I'm all that shocked, but…I guess I am."

Forge of Life was founded in 2013 by controversial tech innovator Jeremy Bélisle. Bélisle, originally born in Paris, grew up in and around New York City. The child of working-class immigrants, he found success through the development of Smoldr in 2010, a dating app exclusively for users with a net worth exceeding $1,000,000. Upon selling the app, Bélisle moved to rural Vermont to establish his health and wellness retreat.

While Forge of Life has advertised itself as a center dedicated to spa-like treatments, the organization has proven controversial to locals in the area due to the growing population living on the property year-round. In 2015, local authorities started receiving reports of loud music being played throughout the night and nude "Forgers," as East Burke residents have termed them, wandering in and out of local businesses.

In recent years, outrage began to surround Bélisle himself. Many former members have come forward accusing Bélisle of sexual assault, blackmail, and manslaughter. While these accusations are currently being investigated by authorities, no active charges have been filed as of this writing.

It is unclear at this time if Bélisle is among the deceased.

On Forge of Life's website, there are scores of testimonials from members of the retreat attesting to the effects of Belisle's teachings.

In one such testimonial, Forge member Kat Summers says, "For me, meeting Jeremy was a clear before-and-after kind of thing. The 'before' I can hardly speak about to this day. And the 'after?' Let me just say that the 'after' is pure bliss."

This is a developing story…

CON AND CONSEQUENCES

JESSICA LÉVAI

GARRETT BARLOW, AUTHOR of the five-volume best-selling fantasy saga *The Ice Warrior* and (until recently) darling of the geek circuit, was on the way to his first public appearance in months. He had spent the last few hours wedged into the back-most seat of a train car, a fedora pulled low over his eyes, doom scrolling on his phone and praying no one would recognize him. Both tasks were successful: No one had disturbed him, and what he read carved a pit into his stomach.

The most painful thing was the email from Bev, his agent. In no uncertain terms she described the mess he'd placed himself in, while nagging him for the pages he promised her before this shitshow began. His eyes were drawn to the last harrowing lines over and over like a hooked fish to the pole.

"I don't need to remind you this con is the last place that will have you. You can become a hermit once it's over. For now, smile. Be nice. And for the love of God, if you screw this up, I will drop you."

Would she? Would Bev say no to fifteen percent of all the sales, the merch, the streaming offers, the comic tie-ins?

Yes. Yes, she would. Bev knew how far his social stock had plunged. She'd been there since the beginning, when he was nobody and she was a hungry baby agent eager to make her mark on the fantasy scene. She was less hands-on these days, but no less astute. She was the one who'd encouraged him to give his title character, Ivar, a best friend: Zaneem, from the Ashai tribe to the south. However, she'd also warned him against subjecting Zaneem to a ghoulish ritual and killing him off. He'd tried to explain his artistic vision to her, just like he tried to explain it to a group of fans who confronted him in a hotel bar. Security intervened, the video went viral, and now there were think pieces on the internet with titles like "*The Ice Warrior* Was Racist Misogynist Garbage From Page One," and "Garrett Barlow Can Fuck Himself Into the Fridge." So, Bev had signed him up for a con in East Nowhere, New Hampshire, to salvage what was left of his fandom and his reputation.

He got off the train and moved as swiftly as he dared through the station, rolling his one piece of luggage behind him. Waiting on the edge of the parking lot was a bearded, middle-aged white guy in jeans and an *Ice Warrior* T-shirt holding a cardboard sign that said CONVENTION in bold black capitals. Garrett extended a hand. "You must be Ed," he said.

"That I am, sir," said Ed Platter, taking the hand and Garrett's suitcase. Ed was the organizer of the con, the one who had reached out to Bev three weeks ago to set this up. "We are just so thrilled you could make an appearance at our little gathering."

"I'm thrilled to be here," said Garrett as he followed Ed to a shiny black pickup truck. Ed tossed the case into the back of the cab and gestured for Garrett to take shotgun. They pulled out of the parking lot and away from the station, away from civilization if Google maps was right. The con site was a two-hour drive away, and already the buildings were thinning and the trees taking over. The summer day was warm, and the sun wouldn't set for a few more hours, but the air conditioner had kicked in as soon as Ed started the truck. Garrett settled into the leather seat and began, finally, to relax.

Ed talked enthusiastically about the con schedule and activities. Garrett tried to listen, but the motion of the car dropped him in and out of a doze.

He startled awake after what his watch told him was more than an hour. Outside the window, squat colonial houses nestled in the green with no sidewalks between them and a few battered lawn signs from the last election hung on for dear life in front. He nearly twisted his neck trying to catch the details of a hunting rifle someone had painted on their garage door. Soon the houses disappeared, and the street became a path through increasingly dense trees.

"First time at an outdoor con?" asked Ed.

"Is it that obvious?" Garrett asked, eyeing the tree cover like it would swallow him.

"A city boy is easy to spot. I promise you; we've got modern facilities on site. No digging holes in the woods."

"That's an image," said Garrett.

The trees blurred and blended. Finally, a dark wooden sign marked CAMPSITE appeared and Ed followed its arrow to the left. "We're here; I just gotta park the truck." Ed pulled into a grove, between another pickup and an SUV. "The site's a quick walk that way," Ed said, indicating with his hand as he put the truck in park. "You hop on out. I'll be around in a second, once I get changed."

Garrett slid off the seat to the ground, stretching his back. A path before him ended in a line of wooden buildings. No doubt these were the "modern facilities" Ed spoke of. Stage fright quickened his pulse. "Hey, Ed?" he called. "What can you tell me about the fans here?"

Ed's muffled voice came from the other side of the truck. "We get maybe two hundred, tops. But true fans. They're going to love you. We hope you'll say a couple words at the feast tonight."

He and Bev—well, mostly Bev—had drafted exactly what he was going to say, and this seemed like a good time to field-test the highlights. "Ed, you know I'm grateful to the fans. All of them. I realize that in trying to explore diversity in the world of *The Ice Warrior*, I've had some fans take offense, and I intend…"

"I'm gonna stop you right there." Ed's voice was sharp, his form still hidden by the truck. "Now, we are well aware of the harassment you've been getting lately, and we think it's a damn shame. You're the author, we're the fans. We're here for the books and we're here for each other." The man emerged from around the truck, wearing a rough tunic, boots, and a fur-lined cloak, in the style of Ivar's people. "*The Ice Warrior* is not canceled here."

"That's terrific," said Garrett, eyeing the ridiculous outfit. What exactly had Bev gotten him into?

FROM THE LINE of buildings a young man appeared, also in an ice warrior's garb, with greenish woad smeared on his cheeks. He waved to Ed, who called out, "Jake! Everything set up?"

"All looks good, Dad," said Jake, embracing his father before stepping back in shock. "Mr. Barlow? This is so cool. I can't believe we really got you."

After a handshake that lasted what felt like thirty seconds, Ed coughed for attention. "Are the warriors ready?"

Jake dropped Garrett's hand, then nodded. "Waiting for your order."

"Awesome. Tell them to stand by and go check on your stepmom. I'm sure she's frantic about tonight."

Jake jogged back. Ed leaned over to Garrett, his fur smelling of sweat and dry-cleaning chemicals. "I have to thank you for introducing me to my wife, Doreen. I mean, we *met* on an app, but when I heard she was a fan of *The Ice Warrior*, I knew she was the perfect woman for me."

Garrett was genuinely touched. He missed hearing stories like this. "That's sweet. Thanks, Ed. I'm glad I could help."

"Your books mean a lot to us," said Ed. He brought himself up taller and shouted, "Ho! Warriors!"

A band of about twenty men, all dressed like Ed in fur and face paint, walked out of the building in formation. They carried weapons and wore armor over their tunics. They stopped in front of Ed and slapped their cuirasses in unison. "Ho! Ivar!" they shouted.

Garrett was struck. He had seen plenty of cosplay in his day, but usually it was pimply nerds with foam swords. The men before him had braided their hair and beards (all real) in the complicated style of Ivar's warriors. The detail on their armor—was that actually tooled leather and scale mail?—took his breath away. The weapons, given the zip-ties holding them in their belts, appeared to be real as well.

"You guys look absolutely amazing," he said. "Really authentic."

The warriors stood at ease, transforming from a troupe of fighters to a clutch of dedicated fans. They surrounded Garrett, shaking his hand, telling him about their favorite characters and scenes. When one asked to have his scabbard signed, the others fell in line behind him, clamoring for the favor. Ed produced a Sharpie and Garrett began. It was the best signing line he'd ever been in. Only one thing was missing.

"Ed," he asked, "What do you say we take some pictures?"

The line went quiet, and every face turned to Ed.

"About that," said Ed, scratching his head. "I'm afraid we don't allow cameras or phones on site. So, I'm going to have to ask you to give me yours, Mr. Barlow. We're trying to recreate Ivar's world, you know, and cameras are distracting."

Garrett fingered the Sharpie. "What if there's an emergency?"

"Nothing your warriors can't handle!" Ed said, to another round of chest-slapping. He leaned in, and the troupe formed a conspiratorial circle. "The other thing is, sir, having a camera at an event like this, someone gets careless on social media, it's just gonna bite you in the ass. Am I right, boys?"

The boys murmured in agreement.

Garrett pulled out his phone; it weighed heavily in his palm. He cast his eye over the very proud, very white men arrayed before him, and understood everyone's desire to keep some things private. It wasn't like cameras had done him any favors lately. "Well, Ed," he said, "That makes a hell of a lot of sense. Here."

The phone disappeared into Ed's cloak. At his signal, the warriors formed an honor guard for Garrett and marched toward the site.

"Thanks so much for understanding," Ed said, picking up a helmet topped with gleaming horns and settled it on his head. "This way, we fans are free to be ourselves."

THE CON TOOK place in an open, grassy area ringed by trees. A row of tents, many modern but plenty of simple cloth and wood, flapped in the breeze on one side, while at the other, costumed fans were hard at work putting tables and benches in place. The feast would begin in about an hour, and the site was already seasoned with the smell of roasting pigs turning lazily on their spits. All around, people were dressed in elaborate garb. Warriors wandered, accompanied by ladies in embroidered gowns, their blond hair twisted into the braids the internet had decided was *the* interpretation of Princess Velle's ceremonial hairdo. Garrett heard snatches of the language he'd created for the books mixed in here and there. It was all blindingly cool.

The first fan to notice his appearance clapped a hand over his mouth to keep from screaming, but it didn't matter. Once Garrett appeared on the site, a madness spread over those attending like a wave. He flinched at first, expecting an egg or a glitter bomb, but his warrior guard kept people a safe distance away and when he listened, all he heard was praise and thanks, and questions about what plans he had for the next book.

"All right, all right!" Ed yelled over the cacophony, and it ebbed. "We all want a piece of him, but let the man breathe." Ed chuckled as fans drew back. "Yeah, save some of that for the festivities tonight, everyone. There's one more person Mr. Barlow has to meet, and then he's ours."

Ed shepherded him through the throng, which parted easily. Garrett bit his lip, afraid he might scream his own excitement. "Ed, this is so incredible," he said.

"I'm glad you like it!"

"I mean, this is what I wanted when I wrote the book." Of course, no one would mistake this cosplay festival for a medieval encampment, but that didn't matter. "These people, they get it. These are the ones I write for."

Ed slapped him on the back and steered him quickly past artisans making costumes and weapons, allowing the odd fan to collect an autograph or gush. Finally, they stopped just before a ring of about fifteen people sitting on the ground. "The Council of Bards," Ed whispered. "What you might call fanfic. They spin their own poems and songs based on your world. I think you'll love them."

This group was clad in the same level of costume as everyone else, but many wore Ashai dress, like Ivar's dead friend Zaneem. Garrett stared uneasily at the circle and declined the invitation to sit. Looking at their faces, he decided it was fair, even appropriate for him to keep moving. The Ashai weren't the focus of the books. At least he could say he had a diverse fan base.

In the center of the circle sat a middle-aged Black woman in Ashai clothing, with a scarlet and gold sash. She held a pencil and marked up a sheaf of paper before her as the others in the circle called out comments. When she noticed Garrett, she smiled and waved him closer. "Mr. Barlow!" she said in a strong voice. "Please, join us!" The other fans in the circle smiled shyly at him. He returned the smile as best he could but kept walking. The woman in the center stood instead and hurried forward to hand him a few sheets of paper. "I'm performing this poem tonight at the feast," she said. "I'm curious to know what you think of it."

God, he hated fanfic. But he stopped and skimmed the text out of politeness. "This is about Zaneem," he said.

"And his murder by Ivar," she replied.

Garrett's stomach tightened. He hoped it was just hunger. "Ivar didn't have a choice. Queen Laera's ritual made Zaneem her puppet. Ivar had to kill him."

"Indeed." She maintained eye contact, as if daring him to say more. The papers shook in his hand. He thought of Bev and took a slow, steadying breath before handing them back. "Well, it's an interpretation."

Garrett almost yelped when Ed guffawed behind him. "Mr. Barlow, I would like to introduce you to my lady, my wife, my co-pilot. This is Doreen, and she's an even bigger fan than I am."

As if to erase any possible misunderstanding, Ed grabbed the poet in a great bear hug and kissed her.

AT LEAST THERE was plenty of beer at the feast. Garrett must have downed three or four tankards of the homemade brew, despite the weird taste. He sat at the high table with Ed and Doreen on one side, Jake on the other. He sulked during the awards for trivia contest winner, cosplay champion and three inductions into the craft guild. Then Doreen stood and recited her poem to the whole crowd.

Her voice demanded attention, even his. Her poem began as an ode to Zaneem, praising his loyalty to Ivar. It spoke of their love, reading way too much into the text. Garrett wondered who in the crowd was supposed to appreciate that. When Doreen recounted Zaneem's horrible suffering on Laera's altar and his death by Ivar's hand, every line felt like an attack. These were *his* characters, not hers. Where did she get off misinterpreting their relationship and judging him, the actual author, for doing what the story demanded?

When it was over, the audience wept real tears. Ed clapped louder than anyone and whistled his approval. Garrett waited for the "true fans" to object, but they never did. Apparently, Ed had lied to him.

Garrett took another pull from his tankard and gagged. What did they put in this stuff? He burped and stood up, wobbling against the edge of the table and barked into Doreen's applause, "I've got something to say!"

Doreen stepped back to give him the floor. If she was angry at his interruption, she revealed nothing. "Please, Mr. Barlow. We're here to honor your creation."

"Yeah, right." He shuffled around Jake's chair and stood in front of the table, in full view of warriors and Ashai alike. "You know, when I first arrived at this con, you greeted me with respect and warmth. And I thought to myself, yes! These people get what *The Ice Warrior* is all about. They make Ivar and Velle proud. They make *me* proud!"

This got a round of applause. Garrett held up his hands to quiet them. It worked. "But some of you don't get it. You're not respectful of the work I put in, or the research I did to create my world. There are people out there who want to inject identity politics into everything, who don't understand that history is what it is, and think they have a right to trample on what other people enjoy."

The crowd was quiet. Sober. They waited.

"Some people asked when the next book is coming out. I gotta say, I don't know. I don't know if it's worth trying to create something if this kind of toxicity is what a writer gets just for telling the truth from his heart." He wobbled again, throwing his arms out to reclaim his balance, if only just. "I don't care who likes my books. I don't care what color you are. But it doesn't give you the right to bully me!"

Ed coughed into the silence. He and Jake had moved from their places at table and now flanked Garrett. "Mr. Barlow, you might want to…"

"What?" Garrett bellowed with all the sting of his betrayal, losing his feet again. Jake's hands on his arms held him up. "What do you have to say?"

Ed sighed. "Nothing. I saw that video. I guess I just didn't want to believe it was true."

"I know, hon," came Doreen's voice behind Garrett. "But it makes the next part easier."

Something solid connected with Garrett's head and the lights went out.

GARRETT WOKE WITH his temples throbbing. He tried to rub his eyes, but his arms were stretched out, his wrists and ankles bound with rough fiber. A hard surface pressed against his shoulder blades. It was full dark now, but torches burned, and by their dim light he could make out the runes on the polished wood structure on which he'd been placed.

He had to admire the craftsmanship that went into a perfect recreation of Queen Laera's altar. These fans were truly dedicated. But he knew what those runes meant, even in his groggy state. He remembered the fans' equally authentic weapons and no-cell-phone policy and felt his stomach sink into the wood.

A foul taste clung to his swollen tongue, and he tried to spit, but it didn't make any difference. Whatever had been in that beer was still working on him. He couldn't speak, but a rustling told him the crowd was still there, gathered around and beyond his eyeline. The indistinct sound collapsed to silence as Doreen approached the altar.

She had changed her costume and was now clad as Queen Laera in a gown of silk and black leather, her spiked headdress stabbing shadows that flickered with the light. She smiled at him, perhaps ruefully, as she checked his ropes and rolled up the sleeve of his right arm.

"Good people!" she called to the crowd. "You know why we are here. This man, Garrett Barlow, has given us a great gift. He created a world we all love and brought us together to celebrate that love. I am grateful, as I am grateful to know each and every one of you." The crowd murmured appreciatively, but there was more. "However, by his decisions, his obstinance, and his refusal to learn from his mistakes, he has tarnished what we cherish.

"Some of you prefer we let him suffer ordinary social consequences. But we know that for every one of us who has been disgusted by his bigotry, others have celebrated him for reinforcing ugly ideas in their own hearts. He has given the worst of his fans permission to be terrible." She paused, swallowing hard. "Even violent."

The crowd murmured in support. Some shouted her name.

Doreen, taking strength from this, continued. "We know how this story goes. We know nothing will stop the movies, the merchandise, or the next book. We fans have to make it right. So tonight, we honor the world that brought us all together. And we celebrate a new beginning in the saga of *The Ice Warrior*. A beginning in which all are welcome, respected, and responsible."

Holy shit, Garrett thought as Doreen pulled an elegant ebony dagger from the sleeve of her gown. *She's going to do the ritual.* He struggled against the ropes and tried to scream, but no sound came out. A hand patted his head. "Take it easy, there," Ed said, still in his horned helmet. "We're gonna take care of everything."

She brought the knife down against the exposed skin of his inner forearm almost gently. The shallow cut burned, blood welling up and dripping on to the altar. Doreen dragged her thumb across the wound and held her hand high, before marking her own forehead with a crimson stripe. One by one, attendees came to the altar. First Ed, who bowed to his wife over Garrett's prone body while she painted his forehead. Then the winners of the trivia and cosplay and crafting contests. Then the rest of them. There were a couple hundred. Would he have enough blood for them all?

"We are the custodians of The Ice Warrior," Doreen said to the faithful as they received the blood on their faces. "We have claimed the knowledge, the art, and the words of this creation for ourselves." The recipients slapped their breastplates or cheered. None looked at him. And none noticed when his head lolled and he lost consciousness.

GARRETT LOOKED LONGINGLY out the window of his room for the hundredth time that day. At least there was a window. Through it he could just make out the edge of the trees. Beyond the trees was a road, and along the road, help. The first week of his imprisonment, he was confident that if he could just reach the road, he could escape. But the fans' superior knowledge of the woods derailed his first escape attempt, and Doreen herself had come to oversee his fitting with the cuff and thick cable that currently chafed his ankle.

"We've separated the art from the artist," she'd said. "Try something like that again, and we'll separate you from your hands."

So, he'd waited. He lost track of the days. He held out hope.

There was a knock at the door. Ed and Jake came in bearing a tray of lunch, which Ed placed carefully on the floor and pushed toward Garrett with his toe. Jake held Garrett's phone, swiping quickly and confidently. The password had only taken him a few hours to crack.

"The Council of Bards'll be by later to read you the new chapter they wrote," said Jake. But I thought you'd want to see something cool first." Jake held up the phone to Garrett's nose so he could read the email:

> *Garrett, these pages are incredible! I love the new direction the series is taking. Can't wait to see more. I think this life of seclusion is working. I'm sorry I doubted you and I promise, I won't come looking for you until you're ready to be found. All the best, Bev.*

"Doreen was real proud of that," said Ed. "Your books are in good hands. We're gonna take care of them, and you, forever."

ARKADIA

MIA DALIA

THEY WORE GARLANDS in their hair. That was the thing I noticed first. Like hippies from a seventies commune. I wanted to drop a sarcastic comment or laugh, but then I glanced at Jay and saw how happy he looked. So, I bit my lip hard enough to taste copper and stayed silent. Looking back on it, that moment of pure, devastating divergence was probably the beginning of the end.

Of the two of us, Jay had always been the seeker. Though we came from similar beige and bland backgrounds and were only a few years apart, he was the one who dreamed in color while I comfortably settled for static. It was part of the initial attraction when we first met—two small-town kids from the Midwest, alone in the big city, trying out college life, playing at being grown-ups. Jay wrote the most beautiful, wildly imaginative stories for our creative fiction class, while I struggled to come up with anything that offered a comfortable departure from autobiographical slices of life.

He chatted me up, charming in his awkwardness, and I fell for it, hook, line, and sinker. We'd been together ever since. The dreamer and the pragmatist. The proverbial opposites who never questioned their attraction, because to do so could invite all manner of potential disappointments. We were a team, determined to stay that way. And because we were so close to each other, it skewed all sense of perspective.

When my employment prospects grew as his dwindled, we simply recalibrated our dynamic as a couple. Jay had always wanted to give writing a serious go, and now he finally had the time to do so. I left him to his research, secretly hoping he'd snap out of it soon enough and rejoin me on the hamster wheel of adulthood.

Instead, Jay found Arkadia.

I raised an eyebrow at him over a plate of overcooked spaghetti. Jay insisted on cooking for us by way of contributing, and I didn't have the heart to tell him I found his culinary efforts barely edible. "As in the mountainous district in the Peloponnese? Or the pastoral paradise, home of the Greek God Pan?"

"Ha."

My affinity for random bits of knowledge and trivia had always delighted him. We were on a college quiz team together, though Jay's specialty tended to be limited to obscure music facts. Mostly, he contributed to the general bonhomie, sort of like a mascot. It had been years since I'd had the brain space for trivia. And my memory was no longer what it used to be.

"It's actually Arkadia. With a K. Named after this guy, the founder. Arkadiy Potemkin." Jay pronounced it carefully, tripping up on the strange syllables.

The last name sounded vaguely familiar. "Polish?"

"Russian."

"Ah." I forked more limp spaghetti into my mouth. Outside of politics, which I was actively trying to avoid, the only thing I really knew about Russia was its beautifully depressing novels I favored as a brooding teen. At seventeen, it all seemed impossibly romantic and tragic. Now, I was lucky to get through a chapter of the latest Agatha Christie knockoff before falling asleep from exhaustion.

"This place, El, it's amazing. They just sort of do their own thing, you know, outside of the society as we know it. And they seem so happy." Jay pushed his hair back. He was getting shaggy, stubbornly refusing to go to the barber, saying he was saving money.

"So, it's a cult?"

"What? No." He laughed and shook his head. "I mean, yeah, I can see how you'd say that, but they are nothing like those places in the TV documentaries. They're more like Christiania, if anything."

My eyebrow shot up involuntarily. "That Copenhagen commune? Didn't that place become dealer's central, attract a lot of gang-related violence, and fall apart?"

"Well, before that," Jay clarified defensively. "When they were good."

"How'd you even find these people?" I asked later, over ice cream, which came from a carton and was impossible to screw up. "Did they try to recruit you or something?"

Jay absolutely will stop and talk to soliciting strangers, inquiring about their causes, apologizing for his inability to contribute, wishing them luck.

"No, they've got a website."

I used to wonder if one day I'd get tired of being the adult in the relationship, of always having to say no, but it hadn't happened yet. For all my faults, my love was a genuinely unconditional article that came with its own well of patience.

"Okay," I said after we finished our supper and the plates were washed, dried, and put away. "Let's see that website."

I had to give it to Arkadiy What's-His-Name. He had presence. Exuding an aura of effortless charm, in one video clip after the next, he introduced himself, his people, and his place (not a cult, *not a cult!*) like some sort of Slavic Brad Pitt. He had piercing blue eyes and a smile to light up any room. Even his Russian accent, usually so harsh in spy movies, was soft with crispy edges, like freshly baked bread.

Keeping his ego in check—and there had to have been an ego, naming a place after himself—Arkadiy spoke of intentional living, creating one's own community, shared values, and other things that to me screamed *cult* and to Jay whispered *home.*

"Do you think we could go check them out?" he asked a few weeks later, making me cringe at the hopefulness in his voice. "Just to see? They offer tours."

This was after my rather tactful, or so I thought, inquiry into whether Jay had found any employment opportunities.

"Nobody wants another desk jokey with a useless English degree, El. And I don't even know if I really want that in my life anymore. I mean, shouldn't we want more? What if it's all just work and work and then we drop dead?"

To be fair, that was exactly what had happened to Jay's dad, who died a month after retirement of a sudden heart attack, taking all his lifelong plans of traveling the world with him.

"There is a very small possibility of that versus a very large probability of living a long life and needing money for it," I countered, taking another bite of food. Jay's spaghetti had finally improved.

"They don't do that in Arkadia," Jay said wistfully.

"They don't work?" I could feel my skepticism skewing my expression.

"No, they do. But not for other people, only for themselves. They grow their own food and make their own clothes and build their own houses and…"

I sighed inwardly, imagining Jay sitting in the house all alone, wasting hours watching Arkadia videos instead of looking at job listings.

He was staying inside more and more. I was gone longer, picking up extra work, trying to keep us afloat. There wasn't enough money or time to go out. I could see Jay building a private echo chamber of one, obsessing over the wrong thing. And I wondered if it would help or harm to go see his obsession in person. Sometimes the best way to end hero worship is to meet the hero.

Jay finally broke me down a few months later, asking for the trip to Arkadia as his birthday present. I couldn't find it in my heart to say no. This was, after all, the same guy who once stayed up all night to get me the tickets to see my favorite band.

Spring was just turning into summer, and the weather on our drive was so beautiful that it was possible to believe we were headed for a fantasy idyll and not a suspicious-sounding, off-grid community.

They treated us like royalty when we arrived, their greetings so genuine, their smiles so broad.

"I'm very glad you could make it," Arkadiy said, his handshake double-handed, warm, callused palms and long, elegant fingers. "Please come in."

It was as if he were a realtor, and we had come to his open house with a suitcase full of cash and no questions asked. My parents didn't show nearly the same enthusiasm when we made the trek down to see them.

"We prepared this for you," Arkadiy said, showing us a small, neatly made-up cabin. "You can stay as long or as little as you like."

I glared at Jay behind our host's back. I didn't care for surprises, and no one had told me about an overnight stay. Jay grinned back in that "come on, you'll like it" way.

We were shown the farmer's stand, the fields that supplied it, the workshops, the library, even a tiny school. They had everything, it seemed: a small self-contained world for a small group of like-minded individuals. And yes, they did seem happy. I tried very hard to gauge if their happiness was of a glassy-eyed, brainwashed variety, but I really couldn't tell.

There was even a lake, small, but picturesque, with a sandy beach on one side and woods on all others. The water shone a strange coppery-red in the midday sun.

Arkadiy noticed me looking. "Looks like blood, doesn't it?" He smiled. "Or, if you're less morbidly inclined, beet juice."

I bent down and put my hand in the lake. My skin looked surreal beneath the red-tinged water.

"It's the local cedars," Arkadiy explained, gesturing all around at the tall trees. Like a proper city person, I knew next to nothing about such things. "They make it look that way."

The red hue made me shudder, but I kept my hand in a while longer, mesmerized by the striking color, wondering what it might taste like but not daring a drink.

In general, it is a very bad idea to drink anything in cults. You can thank Jonestown for that. And yet, by the time we sat down for a communal meal, held outside because of the nice weather, I had given myself permission to live dangerously.

I prided myself on being a good judge of character, and though the jury was still out on Arkadia as a place, I had a fairly strong feeling that none of these people were going to poison us any time soon. I chased down the hearty, vegetable-heavy meals and delicious, freshly baked desserts with homemade lemonade. There were no TVs in sight. No smartphones, no distractions. The conversation flowed. And for a moment, I caught myself thinking that I could get used to that.

When I snapped out of it and looked over at Jay, I could see that he was in thrall of the same thought times a thousand, and it wasn't going to let him go.

We ended up staying for two days and one night, acknowledging the appeal of the place with reluctance on my end and wide-eyed awe on Jay's. Garlands were put in our hair. When it came time to leave, Jay told me he didn't want to. My stomach sank on hearing those words, but part of me had expected it, too.

"Let me just stay here for like a month, trying it out," he pleaded, guilty but determined. "If anything, it'll help me get my head right again. I know I've been so rudderless. I think this is my chance to try and be a better me."

It sounded like a line—perhaps even one of Arkadiy's lines—but I had nothing to counter it with. To me, loving someone meant trying to make them happy. The difficult part was deciding if it ought to be their version of happiness or yours.

In all our years together, Jay and I had never been separated for longer than a few days. Arkadia did not permit cell phones, so our communication was limited to whenever he could find a landline. He even wrote me a handwritten letter, three pages of beautiful sentiments in a barely legible scrawl of someone whose thoughts ran faster than their hands.

Before getting laid off, Jay had had six different jobs while I stayed at the same one, slowly climbing the corporate ladder. He got excited about prospects easily enough but became disappointed just as quickly. That's what I was counting on with Arkadia. I didn't think his fascination with the commune would survive quality time spent there. And I could wait. I had enough patience to counter his impetuous heart.

Jay stopped calling after three weeks. Whenever I dialed the number for the last landline he'd used, it just rang and rang. Each tone sounded more and more like a shriek of an alarm.

My best office friend, Cindy, suggested I speak to her husband, a police detective.

"Legally, there's nothing to be done," he told me over coffee. "Your husband's an adult, there of his own volition."

"That we know of," I pointed out.

He pursed his lips and gave me a look.

"Please," I said, playing the helpless card. "I'm really worried."

He sighed, chewing on the corner of the mustache Cindy was always complaining about.

"Email me everything you know about this place, website, the guy's name, location, et cetera. I'll look into it," he said eventually, obviously pushing through his reluctance for Cindy's sake.

I thanked him profusely, paid for our coffees, went home, and sent him all the info I had. Then I waited.

There was, of course, the option of driving down to Arkadia myself, but the prospect of in-person confrontation scared me more than I cared to admit. While I wanted to know that Jay was alive and safe and not in the clutches of some evil manipulator, I wasn't quite ready to face the potential reality of being abandoned by the love of my life for something better.

It was like that saying, "If you love someone, let them go…" I wanted Jay to come back to me of his own free will, not be dragged back by guilt and obligations.

It took another week to realize that Jay had reversed-mortgaged our house and emptied our joint bank account. I sat stock-still, staring at the computer screen in disbelief that was quickly turning to red-hot anger, as my phone rang.

"Yes?" I hissed after mashing the green button with my thumb.

"It's Detective Johnson."

I couldn't think, couldn't respond.

"Paul. Cindy's husband," he offered as if sensing my confusion.

I took a deep breath and let it out. "Hi, Paul."

"I wish I had some good news for you," he said in a tone flattened by years of experience in delivering the bad kind.

The drive back to Arkadia on my own felt endless. When I got there, I found exactly what I expected to find: nothing.

I walked the empty grounds that suddenly seemed wrongly sized without any people, like an apartment you can hardly recognize without all your furniture in it.

The cabins must have been of a flatpack variety, easily taken down to be reassembled elsewhere. The only one that remained, built of genuine wood, was the cabin where we had stayed. I pushed the unlocked door and entered it. There was nothing in it save for a wilted garland on the floor.

If Jay was here, I'd tell him that I finally remembered where I had heard the name Potemkin.

A Russian minister and a lover of Catherine the Great, he had famously, and perhaps apocryphally, built fake portable villages along the coast of Dnieper River to impress the Empress and her guests on her trip to Crimea.

All facades and warm glowing fires. All a lie.

But Detective Johnson had told me that Arkadiy was more than a liar. And Jay was not the only dreamer he had hooked with that easy charm and fake promises. Come to think of it, were his eyes even blue? In the photo Paul texted me—the website had disappeared without a trace—they looked gray. Like steel. Like a stormy sky.

I waited for the police to arrive as I sat by the nameless lake. The reflected sky looked surreal in the cedar-red water.

The sirens dopplered closer. Soon, I was surrounded by men in uniform, talking about dragging the lake.

A stout middle-aged man with a florid face introduced himself to me as the local sheriff.

"Can't believe this happened right under our noses," he said, shaking his head and gesturing to the water.

"The water's red because of the cedars," I told him.

He shook his head. "You city folk. Look around. Those are spruce trees. That water is red because…"

I stopped listening to him. A heart can only take so much. The wind rippled the surface of the lake, bringing with it a faintly ferrous smell.

#IDeserveIt

CAT DELANI

TOMORROW IS MY Slashr-versary.

One year spent trying to be victimized.

What am I doing wrong?

I pull up my profile on the Slashr app and drop another pin. It's my third one this hour, but I've been walking pretty fast, so they're spaced out. And with all these back alleys, it's not exactly an easy trail to follow. Still, though. Do I look too desperate? Is it not fun to target me if I'm asking for it this much?

I scroll back to the start of my profile, back when I was trying hard *not* to ask for it. When I was trying to be someone's final girl. It works for some people, I know. I've seen it. Those gloating photos, covered in blood. Fulfilling someone's fantasy of dying at the hands of their perfect chosen partner. Didn't work for me, though.

I swipe quickly through all the chaste photos, the volunteering updates. What a waste of time. I wasn't cut out to be one of them, clearly. So, I had to change tactics. I tried befriending other users. Some people want to cut through a pack, right? Slashers can't resist a party. I was never at the right ones even though I was close, once.

I land on that photo, my one pathetic battle scar. I'd taken a knife to the arm. He wasn't even aiming for me, but I pretended he was. I look at my caption, "Anyone want to finish the job?" and grimace at the comments. Plenty of knife emojis, blood emojis. Empty threats. Empty, because, well. I'm still here. One comment in particular sticks out, though.

"Why do you want them to?"

It's from a girl with the handle, @smiley_riley. Definitely a final-girl type. Even has that gender-neutral name going for her. But most interesting is that this comment is new. From a few hours ago, even. I must have missed the notification, focused as I've been on trying to die today. I should pay better attention. What if a killer wants to play?

I click through to her profile, and, yeah, I was right. She's *pristine*, tall and lean, with sun-kissed, naturally blonde locks. She has a lot of beach photos, all in tasteful coverups of course. No bikinis here, can't risk the cleavage. What's this kind of girl doing commenting on an extra's profile in cloudy Seattle? Unless…did she move?

I look at her profile more closely. She *has* dropped pins around Seattle. Visiting, maybe? Ugh, why are the final-girl wannabes always so damned coy? I know they must be; they have to appear in all ways innocent because otherwise, they aren't worth killing. Like me, I guess. Not worth killing at all.

Why is it so fucking hard to get killed these days?

I should have been born earlier. Where all I had to do was be a co-ed and have long brown hair, right? But what did those lucky girls do? They cut their hair. They dyed it. How could you be so ungrateful? To be the type of girl someone wants to kill and…ruin it?

The rage is building up, again. How unfair it all is. *This* is why I could never be a final girl. Final girls, they want to live. They have that drive to survive at any cost. And the unfairness that makes *them* angry is watching innocent people die.

I stopped trying to be innocent a while back.

And that's what makes it so unfair. I have worked hard for this. I *deserve* it. A knife across my throat. Or, better, spilling my guts. Cut me open, expose me. I need to pay. Back at the top of my profile, now, I read my bio:

Krista, 23F. Girls bullied: 8. Boys teased: 17. People fucked: 29. I got my boss fired. I stole rent from my roommate. #ideserveit

And above that, a messy, topless, selfie. How to die in a horror movie 101: Take off your shirt, then have sex. Or be a mean girl—that's a good way to draw righteous ire, too.

Listing your counts, or how many people you've hurt, is new, a trend started by younger users. Is that it, am I too old now? You're not supposed to lie about your age. But should I change it? I'm trying so hard. I'm about to click that edit button when a notification comes through, "@smiley_riley liked your photo."

Her again? I click on it before the banner disappears. It's my most recent photo, the one I just took showing off how easy I would be to kill in this alley. I even posed next to a Dumpster, easy disposal, yeah? That's how I captioned it, too. "Throw me away." I don't even need to see the notification.

"You're not trash."

The bitch even added a heart emoji.

I click through to her profile again. She's added a new photo, at a coffee shop. A Seattle coffee shop. Just a few minutes away. I could walk over there and watch her. If anyone's final-girl hunting today, maybe I can be the one to take that knife to the throat, can be one of the party after all–the blood sacrifice. The opening kill.

There's no other role left for me.

That's the slippery slope. Once you make one wrong decision, have one flaw, well, you give up on being a final girl. You can never go back because you're not perfect anymore. Not that I ever was. Probably why I couldn't hack it. But the more rules you break, the earlier you die, and I've been breaking every rule I can. I drink. I smoke. I sleep around. Guys, girls, whatever. I'm not sure it matters as much these days, but I want my bases covered.

Vandalism is my version of a prank. I can't exactly be in on a true prank, not without a friend group to laugh about it with. And, well, making friends on this app isn't going so well. Should I add the pranks to my profile? Tires slashed: 24. Windows smashed: 35. Phone lines cut: 6.

Each one is a whispered plea: Do this to me. Do this to me. I deserve it.

My finger is back on that edit button again.

I close the app, instead. Turn my feet toward the coffee shop. I don't even have to get too close to see her—@smiley_Riley. The sunlight is reflecting off her hair, because she's sitting in the window, watching the street. Of course. She needs to be vigilant, after all. Worse, though, she's waving, smiling–at me. I turn around, just to check. No one there, not even a masked murderer, unfortunately.

Is she waiting for me?

She waves again, this time with her drink, somehow not spilling the green-tinged froth over the side. Is she the real deal, then? Actually perfect? Fucking annoying. Why did I even come here? Why did I need to see her? I better die for this.

I force a smile to let her know she's been seen. Walk slowly to the door of the little shop, making sure not to check down the alley between us just in case someone wants to ambush me. Please. But they don't. Another disappointment. The bell above the door jingles as I enter. The smell of coffee and pastries spills briefly out into the street, along with some hipster singing about the ocean.

It's that kind of coffee shop. Entirely the wrong genre for me and what I'm looking for. This is where I'd go if I was using a dating app, not a killing app. I want a partner, yeah. Someone to spend the rest of my life with, true. It's just that I want that sentence counted out in breaths and blood spurts, instead of years. I thought I'd find them before now. Or rather, I thought they'd find me.

But no one is chasing me. No matter what I do I guess I'm not worth the effort. I couldn't even get killed the normal way—one-night stands with strangers. Those hookups weren't *safe*. They'd fuck me, sure. Sometimes even in a dark alley, perfect for a knife, but no one could offer that commitment. And tomorrow marks one year of putting myself out there. I'm running out of time.

Smiley Riley meets my eyes. Smiles at me, again. It's in her name for a reason, I guess. She stands up, gestures with her head toward a booth, somewhere quieter. That's when I see she's got another drink with her. She got me coffee? I follow her to the back booth, slide in across from her, and take the drink. It's still hot. She ordered this recently, like she knew I was coming.

It's like she was watching my location on the app. My breath catches, but I hide it with a sip. It's my drink—black coffee—which she would only know if she was watching me for a lot longer than just today. Did you come to town for me, final girl?

"So, why do you want to die?"

Well, it's a little rude to buy someone a coffee if you're going to make them spit it out, Smiley Riley. That's pretty fucking forward of you. I flip her question around.

"Why do you?"

"I don't."

She's still smiling, too. Maybe it's a joke. It's got to be. I mean, even the final girls like her kind of want to die, right? Who signs up for Slashr without at least a little death wish? But that smile, it's like she knows something.

Maybe she really *is* a killer? Good ploy, a fake final-girl act. Has that been done? I mean outside of the movies. We've all seen *Scream 4*. I'm talking about on the app. Can you have a killer profile and a victim one? Can you just switch roles like that?

Could *I* switch roles like that?

I size her up. She's taller than me. More fit, which is a given. But she doesn't view me as a threat. I see it in her eyes. Predator or not, she knows I'm prey. It's all I've wanted to be. For the past year, I've dedicated my life to finding someone who would want to kill me, but what would it feel like to find someone to kill, instead?

"Krista?"

Her smile doesn't slip, her eyes are so full of concern. She even looks fucking genuine.

"I just want to matter to someone."

It's an honest confession, and I hope it lands. Hope she doesn't see that I'm scanning this coffee shop for weapons. Trying this new idea on. I've never bothered with carrying a knife or anything. What would I want to defend myself from?

"You matter to me."

I know I do, Smiley Riley. The question is, why? Are you really a final girl, caring about everyone? Do I matter to you because you've got a knife under this table, just waiting to drive it home? Or do I matter to you because I'll be the one who takes your life?

The tension between us stretches thick. Like how it feels before you kiss someone. If you like them, if it means something. If that kiss holds the promise of a future. A life. And not one spilling out of you in red. I wonder what it'd be like—to want that.

"You don't know me," I say.

I can't help picturing her killing me. How would she do it? Or… has she already done it? Has a slasher ever killed with poison, before? I take another sip of my coffee, watching her over the rim. It only tastes like coffee. And no, I don't think they would because it'd be too impersonal. You better not have poisoned me, Smiley Riley. I'll be insulted.

"I know enough. I know you're lost. That you're lonely. Hurting. You must be running from something horrible to go to such lengths."

Who the fuck does this bitch think she is? What, just because I want to die I must be *sad?* Because I'm looking for my perfect partner, I must be *lonely?* No. Fuck you, Smiley Riley. You don't get it. Why are you even here? Why are you even on Slashr if you don't belong?

I don't say any of that, though. I have a role to play. I rub my eye, hard. Making sure to smear my makeup, so it looks like there could have been tears at play. Tears I don't want to spill. I look around the coffee shop, like I'm embarrassed.

"I don't want to…talk about it here."

Buy it, final girl.

I look down into my maybe-poisoned coffee, forcing myself not to watch her reaction. Still half-hoping for a blade against my thigh, cutting into my femoral artery, spilling blood instead of fake tears.

"You live around here, don't you?"

I look up, now, hope swelling in my chest until I can feel it shining in my eyes. I'll be alone with her soon. I nod, already standing. She gets up and follows me. My heart thrills more. She's following me back to my place. Maybe even to kill me. It's what I always wanted.

I lead her to my home like walking in a dream. When we get there, I realize I forgot to hope someone jumps out from every alley. I didn't think to drop a pin. I do have my usual fantasy of being pulled backward down the stairs by my hair. She doesn't do that, though. And I'm surprisingly grateful. I want to get her inside. I want to see where this goes.

We finally reach my floor, entering my apartment through the always unlocked door.

"Hello?"

I have to say it every time. You know, just in case. Smiley Riley stops in the doorway.

"You don't lock your door?"

Aw, did I actually surprise you?

I make my way into the kitchen, checking my knife block. All weapons are accounted for. But that's good because I want her to myself.

"Why lock it when I want the bad guys to come in?"

I'm leaning against the sink when she comes in. The click of the lock still echoing behind her footsteps tells me she wants me all to herself, too.

"Wow, you're deeper into this than I realized. Did something happen at home, when you were little? Is that what you don't want to talk about?"

What is she, a fucking therapist? Or is she getting off on this? Does she like to play with her food? She's standing across from me now. In my tiny hallway of a kitchen, we're almost touching. My eyes flick over to the knife block again—force of habit.

Two knives are missing now.

So she grabbed one, too, then. Does she know I have one? Or does she assume I keep the missing one elsewhere—by my bed, perhaps?

My heart could burst. This is thrilling. I feel *alive.* If I knew living could feel like this, I wouldn't have wasted so much time trying to die. Which means I have to move fast.

"It was my mom," I start. I'm bending over, like this hurts to admit. But that's just to hide that I'm pulling the knife from behind my back. I don't hesitate before I slip it into her ribs. It's surprisingly easy to cross that line. It's less easy to drive it home. The blade scrapes over bone and sends a shiver through my arm. I feel the vibration in my teeth.

In the span of a few breaths, my life changes forever. Her blood is spilling over my hand. The warmth is better than any hug. The joy is so sharp it hurts. I look up into her face, and she's still smiling.

My Smiley Riley.

The knife falls from her hand, and I see it's red, too. Did she get me? I can't feel it. I'll worry about that later. I need to be with her as the light leaves her eyes. It's what she deserves. I'm the most important person to her, now.

And I always will be.

THE GIG

CORY SWANSON

I PULL UP in a car that costs less than the instruments I'm hauling in it. Isn't that the joke? What's the definition of a musician? Someone who pulls up in a two-thousand-dollar car hauling ten-thousand dollars' worth of instruments. Ba-dum-ching.

I'm nervous. A week ago, some guy called me about this gig. He named only a time, a place, and a price. I have no idea what to expect or even what music to play. Jesus, I don't even know if I dressed right.

Thank God for cigarettes.

This place is marvelous, and I stare out the windshield in awe. It's a castle—a literal castle—built on top of a hill in the middle of Colorado's ranch land. I'm intimidated by its grandeur. Is this what I would do if I had that kind of money? No, I'd probably buy another guitar. Maybe two. This is the kind of house you build when you have more money than you could ever spend. And then of course you're always searching for ways to show it off. Houses, cars, jewelry.

Musicians.

I toss my cigarette out the window and grab an armload of gear from the back. An unplaceable fear creeps down my spine. It's more than nerves; it's a feeling like I shouldn't even go inside. This is what I do, though. Rich people hire me to come play for their events. I show up, I suck up to them, I "ooh" and "aah" at their houses, I play some tunes while everyone ignores me—aside from polite applause when I stop—then I grab a free glass of Chianti, collect my check, and leave.

The gravel that crunches under my shoes glows pale in the moonlight as I approach the castle. It feels like the kind of night Dracula might answer the door. I've never met these people. They said they were friends of another guy who hired me to play a while back. I had tonight free, so I accepted the gig as one does.

"What kind of music do you want me to play?" I'd asked on the phone.

"We'll go over that when you get here."

"But I want to prepare. I want to give you your money's worth."

"It's an improv gig. Do you improvise?"

I almost backed out at that point, but for the money they were offering, I'd ride a damned unicycle if I had to. "Yes. I improvise. All the time."

"Good. I'll send you directions. Be here by ten."

So now I'm here, knocking on the door. There are no lights on and I wonder if I've got the wrong place. *Impossible*, I think. *How many castles can there be out here?*

Just as I'm about to turn away, the door opens. "Ah, Leo," a man says. He's wearing a button-down linen shirt with the collar undone. He has a toothy, glowing grin and the fabled glass of Chianti in his hand. "I'm so glad you're here. Come, let me show you where to set up. Is this all your gear?"

"No," I say. "I need to go back and get my amp and my board."

The castle's interior is grand beyond compare. Guests mill about beyond the foyer beneath high, bent beams that hold up the ceiling like that of a cathedral. The floors and walls are stone, and display works that I am sure are originals from the Renaissance. My guts twist. I want to live in a place like this. I want to own a Rubens. Or two.

I glance around, looking for a place set aside for me. I don't find one. The guests are talking and eating hors d'oeuvres on one end of the room, and rows of folding chairs are set up at the other. There's a man walking around with a bag and guests are sticking their faces in it, taking deep breaths. At first, I think they're all throwing up their food into the bag, some sort of rich person bulimia thing, but I realize it's probably drugs.

"Here," my host says, opening a door off to the side that leads to a modest bedroom.

"Is this the dressing room?"

"No, this is where you'll set up."

I panic. What kind of party is this? I'm playing in a bedroom? Will I be accompanying two lovers?

"Well?" my host says.

"I, um, this isn't what I was expecting."

"Indeed."

"I can't stay out in the main room to play for your guests?"

"This is where I'd like you to set up."

I consider walking out but then remember what he promised to pay me. I swing my guitar case off my shoulder and set it against the bed. "Can I get a glass of Chianti?"

"Of course," my host says. "Why don't you go get the rest of your gear and I'll have your drink waiting for you."

Back outside, my mind is abuzz. I've played some strange gigs before. One night, I was asked to bring my djembe and wear all black. When I got there, they gave me a silver mask to wear. I marched down a hall with a team of feathered dancers, then stood by a door drumming while several dignitaries paraded through. I saw the mayor and the governor go by. When I collected my check, the event organizer told me to keep the mask.

But this… I'm going to play in a bedroom while the party keeps happening in another room? Why don't they just crank up their stereo? One of them has to have Spotify. They live in a castle; they can afford the premium, ad-free service.

I smoke another cigarette on my way to and from my car as I laugh to myself. *It's a living,* I think.

What are they going to be doing while I play that they don't want me to see? Is this an orgy? Or are they some satanic cult, and they're going to sacrifice a goat on the stone floor?

I let myself inside this time, hauling my amp to the bedroom, saying, "Excuse me," over and over to part a path in the crowd.

My host is in the bedroom, running cords under the door to a small television set. "Your drink is on the bed stand," he tells me, not looking up from his work.

My wine is in carved crystal stemware, and it sits on a coaster that appears to be solid mother of pearl. I take a long drink. I'm going to need it.

"Put your amp outside the door so we can hear it."

I nod, still wondering why I can't be out there to play. "What's the TV for?" I ask, unwinding my cords.

"I want you to accompany what you see on it," he says.

"Oh, like a silent movie?"

"Yes."

"I wish you would have sent it to me ahead of time. I could have come up with something great to play."

My patron scowls. "It doesn't work like that. The material doesn't exist yet."

I scoff in disbelief.

"You claimed you were able to improvise over the phone."

"I am."

"Then that's what I'm asking you to do."

I take a deep breath. "Yeah. Okay. I'll be ready in a couple minutes."

After I have my gear plugged in, I tune up my guitar. I'll be able to pull something out of my ass, I'm sure, but I'd love it to be good. What if I play smooth jazz and they're out there sacrificing a goat? I wish I had just a little more information.

"Are you ready?" my host asks, returning to the room.

I glimpse a thick braid of wires heading out from the TV and under the door. *Why the hell did he hook up so many feeds to this TV?* "Um, what genre do you want me to play?"

"Whatever comes to your mind as you watch the images on the screen," he says.

"But, I mean, what are you guys into? I don't want to pull out a death metal improv when you guys were hoping for some Kenny G tunes."

"Whatever you come up with will be fine, I assure you. It's a stream-of-consciousness thing. Be as creative as you like."

"Okay," I say, but my brain is thinking, *moron*. "Get me some water and I'll be ready to go."

Within the minute, a caterer brings me a single glass on a tray and takes my empty. I nod my thanks, drinking deep.

The door clicks shut and the light in the bedroom turns off. The twinkling LEDs of my effects pedals are the only illumination I have.

Through the door, I can hear my host giving a speech. "Thank you all for coming. I, for one, have been looking forward to this experience for quite some time."

Definitely an orgy, I think, and I get my wah-wah pedal ready.

"I want to thank Mr. Gillibrand for making this all possible," my host's voice continues, followed by light applause. "Without him, this visionary technology would never have come to be. I also want to thank Leo, who will be accompanying our experience with his musical stylings. He's in the bedroom there so as not to disturb our proceedings. Be sure to express your thanks to him at the end of the evening."

Another round of light applause erupts.

"Now, there are plug-ins next to each of your chairs. Go ahead and connect to your interfaces and we'll get started."

What are they plugging into? I wonder. This doesn't jive with my orgy theory. I realize I might need to go more electronica, and I get my delay pedal ready.

There's a long silence and I start to wonder if they're waiting on me. "I'm ready," I say.

There's no response. *Should I start?*

Just as I'm about to say screw it and begin playing something, anything, the screen flashes to life.

There's a house surrounded by a green lawn. It's a beautiful day. There's no sound, but there would be birds chirping if there were. *Okay,* I think. *I can do this.*

I turn off all my effects and strum a folksy little tune on a clean feed. My amp is audible but muffled by the door. That part doesn't bother me as much as not being able to read the crowd's reaction. Are they all watching this, too? Are they digging it? There's no way to tell.

The camera circles the house, then travels up. *Drone footage,* I think. The scene becomes more grand, there are mountains in the background. I hit my looper and the folk riff continues as I layer on a soaring, overdriven line.

Okay, I'm feeling it.

The camera heads into the hills, traveling out over the forest. The hills are covered in snow. We bank in and out as though we're an eagle until we come upon a clearing. Below us is a pack of wolves closing in on an elk herd.

I've got this, I think, dropping into a suspenseful, delay-heavy riff. I'm loving it, even though I'm totally ripping off Pink Floyd's *Echoes.*

The camera comes in close. I can't believe the drone isn't bothering the wolves or the elk, but the hunt is on, I suppose. Maybe they're used to human noises.

A wolf has an elk with a limp in its sights. Within seconds, we're right there with it, tearing at the elk's neck.

Jesus, I think. *That got real fast.*

I switch on the overdrive and pull out a galloping metal riff I've been workshopping. *No time like the present for this one.*

The other wolves join in, sinking their teeth into the elk's flesh. Blood soaks the snow and steam rises from our jaws.

I blink. Not my jaws. The wolves' jaws. *Am I hallucinating? Was there something in that glass of wine?*

The scene is hard to watch. The wolves are fighting over intestines, tugging at limbs with their powerful maws. One reaches out a hand—

A hand?

—and snaps a leg joint. He stands on two legs, holding his prize above his head and howling.

I blink again. *Christ, what is this movie?* My playing becomes wilder, a frenzy of looped layers and special effects.

The movie continues, one bizarre scene after another. The wolf-men are a common thread, but the camera, still in a single shot, travels around, showing how these creatures live among us, unknown. There's fire, heroic deeds. I'm no longer sure how it's all connected.

My hands become sore. It feels as though I've been playing for hours. I want to sneak a peek at my watch, but it's dark and doing so would cause a break in the music.

Had my host given me an end time? I search my memory, but

all I can recall is the start time. It has to be well past midnight now.

This is insane.

How will I know when to stop?

Will it stop?

What are the guests doing?

Are they just sitting out there watching this crazy shit?

Thoughts of an orgy flash in my head again. That has to be it, doesn't it? They're on some crazy drug and they're doing their thing while watching this insane movie.

Could still be a ritual sacrifice too, considering the film's content.

Time passes and my curiosity mounts. The temptation to peek outside the door is becoming unbearable.

The movie has devolved into a swirling maelstrom of colors. It looks like those close-up pictures of Jupiter sent back by unmanned spacecraft. The thought occurs to me that I've got my looping pedal hooked up. I can put up to thirteen sound layers in, and they'll just keep repeating. Seeing as the image on the screen is static now, I work in a few more layers and sneak my guitar off my shoulder, laying it on the bed.

I tiptoe to the door, careful not to trip over any cords. My hand on the knob, my heart pounds. *What am I going to see if I open this door? Will I be in trouble? Will I be an accomplice to whatever's going on?*

What if it's a murder? My God, with all I saw on that screen, I wouldn't be surprised. Then what? *Do I really want to do this?*

I can't take it anymore. I have to know.

I turn the doorknob as slowly and quietly as I can. Whatever's going on, I don't want to disturb it.

The gap between the door and the jamb widens one inch, two. A pale, dim light comes from the other side.

My breath not quite under control, I sneak an eye into the gap, my looping tracks still churning through my amp.

At first, I think they're all dead. The guests are sitting in various states of motionless repose in their folding chairs, their bodies drooped and slack. There's no blood, but for a moment I'm sure they're dead. The terror fills me, but I manage to choke back the scream.

Then I notice something. There's no movie screen. However, each guest has a cord plugged into their head. Two old-school RCA jacks, red and white, hidden in their hair just behind their temples.

The cords all snake into the master braid that leads under the door to my TV.

I gape. The scene is too much for my brain to handle. I can't move. *What the hell is going on?*

"Can I help you?" a voice whispers next to my ear.

I jump and choke off the urge to scream. My host is standing to my right. "I, um…I just." I notice the RCA jacks sticking out from his now-disheveled hair.

"Everyone is okay. Don't worry," he whispers.

I'm paralyzed.

"They're sleeping."

"Where's the TV?"

"It's their dream."

"But are they…?"

"They're not dead. Just a few more minutes, Leo. I'll come get you when it's over."

One of the guests gets up, his pose not unlike the wolf I saw onscreen earlier. Two large men—security?—emerge from the shadows and close in on his seat, but before they can get there, he's tearing at his neighbor's chest with his fingernails. Now there's blood. A melee ensues, the large men wrestling him down, but the other guests are undisturbed, still catatonic in their seats.

The host guides me back to my room and pushes the door closed with eyebrows raised. I attempt to collect myself, strapping my guitar back on.

The scene on the television is moving away from Jupiter, passing on into the cosmos. The night sky is twinkling. It's calm in a way I'm not. My body is almost throbbing with anxiety.

I thin out the layers on the looper until all that's left is me playing that folksy riff from the beginning. The stars fade and I pull back the volume.

Then, finally, everything goes black, and I stop playing.

The light in the bedroom turns back on. Somehow, there's a new glass of water sitting on the bed stand for me. I'm too bewildered to question how it got there, and I take a deep drink.

"So, what did you think, ladies and gentlemen?" the host's voice booms from the other side of the door.

The guests cheer, an eruption of sound in stark contrast to the silence of a few moments earlier.

"And what about Leo and his guitar stylings?"

More applause.

My door opens and I'm standing there with my guitar around my shoulder. I take a bow, not knowing what else to do. The crowd hollers their approval.

"On behalf of the Dream Collective, I thank you for being here tonight. Drive safe and check the website for updates."

There's a noisy chatter as the crowd gathers their coats and purses. "Wonderful job," the occasional patron leans in the bedroom to say.

"Thank you," I respond graciously every time, wondering what happened to the guy who lost it and how they got it cleaned up so quickly. Did anyone else even notice?

Later, as I'm winding up my cords, the host comes in with his checkbook out. "Wonderful work," he says.

"Oh, well, thank you. I wasn't too heavy handed?"

"Oh, not at all. Would you be available for another job two weeks from now?"

"Yes—" I begin out of habit. "Wait. Can you tell me what that was?"

"Ah, well, it's kind of a secret. I wouldn't want it getting out," he says as he fills out my check.

"Look, man, I saw what I saw, okay? And the guy who lost it. Is everyone okay?"

"Listen," he says, parting his hair behind his temple to show his own RCA jacks. "There were a lot of powerful people here tonight. If you know what's good for you, you'll take the check and keep your mouth shut."

"But…why are you doing this?"

He taps the company name in the upper left-hand corner of the check as he hands it to me. "Dream Collective," it reads. "So that we might dream as one," he says, quoting the company slogan printed in the watermark. "You'll notice I wrote the check for more than I promised. You can expect similar payments at future engagements."

My eyes are wide, but I fold the check and place it in the pocket of my shirt. "I'm available in two weeks."

"Wonderful," he says.

"One more question." I can't help myself. "Why do you need me? Why not just pipe in some music on your stereo? Or through the cords?"

"The jacks are only hooked to our ocular nerves, and random music would not mold and bend to the events in our heads."

I nod like I understand. I don't.

The host clears his throat. "Well, two weeks. Same time, same place."

I nod, shouldering my guitar case and gathering a handful of gear. I've had weird gigs before, and I know one thing for sure: At some point, you put that check in your pocket and you stop asking questions.

WE CONTAIN MULTITUDES

ANDREW KOZMA

I FIRST NOTICED George Slavinia hitting on women at Poison Girl, my neighborhood bar. Poison Girl wasn't a big, cattle-call kind of place you could get lost in, and it wasn't expensive, either, where you paid your money to be seen and left alone. It was a dive, or it wanted to be, or it pretended to be, which made its local flavor that of an expensive whiskey you'd poured the night before but never finished. Those who didn't like the atmosphere never came back, returning to the ever-changing storefronts of Midtown or Washington. Those who did like the atmosphere, they never left.

George was a semi-regular who had the sort of attractiveness that puts hooks in your eyes. I don't usually swing that way, toward prettiness with an edge, but even I couldn't keep my attention from straying back to him. He was the shiniest thing in the dimly lit bar, his entire personality the too-bright whiteness of a fresh-snapped bone. From all the way down the long, crowded bar I could hear his seductive whisper, and though he aimed his efforts at just one woman, every ear in the place was tuned to his lilting drawl.

Honestly, Poison Girl isn't the place to go for a one-night stand. The bar is all regulars and the occasional lost soul. Even on weekends, the people from the suburbs have all been here before. Everyone knows everyone else's name, or at least fakes a passing familiarity. But on that night, George unerringly honed in on one of the few lost souls there, a woman named Regina who was evolving into a regular.

"Your eyes are berries," he told her. "No one's ever told you that before, have they?"

She shook her head, eyes fixed on her chewed-up fingernails. He covered those chewed-up nails with his hands, and it was like they suddenly didn't exist.

Ricky, the red-haired bartender, was washing glasses in the sink on my end of the bar. Without looking up, he muttered, "No one ever told her that because it's a stupid thing to say. What kind of berries, even?"

I laughed quietly in agreement, but I understood what George was doing. Sure, it seemed crass and overblown to others, but under that gaze, with eyes so intense they burn straight through your skin to your core, it reveals the childlike you hiding in the center of your grown-up body, the one who always dreamed this could happen. It didn't matter that Regina's eyes were nothing like berries, but more like baker's chocolate, and she knew it. Those sorts of compliments work to remake you in someone else's eyes, which remolds you in your own head, your self-image painted anew by another's brush. It's hard not to glory at finding yourself in someone else's dreams, especially if you're lost.

And Regina was lost.

George's compliments overwhelmed her, even if she didn't believe half the things he said. As she leaned into him, I could imagine her thinking to herself that the truth is overrated. That sometimes all we want—all we need—is a little fantasy.

Happy Hour ended, and with it the sun went down. The bar had begun to hum with more than just the downtown office drones having their after-work drink and the service industry crowd pre-gaming for a night full of self-centered customers who barely registered waiters and bartenders as human. All the added noise meant I couldn't overhear how George was seducing Regina anymore, but I kept my eye on them as their body language grew increasingly cursive.

A suited man sat next to me and opened some Bukowski on the bar top, then pretended to ignore me. I played along, drifting my eyes into his orbit until he broke the silence too casually. Fifteen minutes later, I looked up from the conversation and George and Regina were gone, vanished into the night.

Regina had moved to Houston from New Jersey, which she described as a black hole of the soul, powered by the soulless. There, she worked for day traders in New York City, cleaning their mansions in the Jersey suburbs. In Houston, she took all the money knowledge she learned on the sly from them—her employers treating her as a sounding board for all their plots and plans, dismissing her either because she was a woman or because she was hired help, she didn't know and didn't care, not anymore—and she made bank in her new city. But she'd left her family and her friends behind. "Good riddance to all of them," she'd say before taking her first shot of the evening. That shot was a different cheap whiskey each time. Though she could buy much better quality stuff now, she wanted to remember what it was like when the worst was all she could afford. She didn't let anyone buy her drinks and, before George, the attention of most men had as much hold on her as fog.

I never saw Regina again.

George became a semi-regular. The bartenders always took his order, served his drinks, accepted his payment with the bare minimum of conversation. The worst thing to happen to someone at a neighborhood bar was for everyone to ignore him, which they did. Regulars circled together if he came near like a herd blocking off a predator. Some even broke that rule of standard bar friendliness, like when Alejandro bought a round for everyone on the night of his bachelor party, then pointed to where George sat at the middle of the bar, a moat of empty space around him, and yelled, "Except him!"

No one paid attention to George. In fact, everyone actively tried *not* to pay attention to him.

But I watched him. I studied him. For me, he was like a frozen river on the verge of shattering into motion. I couldn't look away for fear I'd miss someone else dropping through the ice into the cold depths below.

I didn't have long to wait. Two weeks after Regina, I entered

Poison Girl to find George huddled around another woman. From her short, spiked black hair I knew it was Linh, a regular who'd slid backward into being a lost soul.

George's arm was around her shoulder in an awkward way, but one that undeniably declared THIS IS MINE to everyone watching. And since everyone was already used to ignoring George, they ignored Linh as well, people rolling their eyes at her, muttering, "He's her problem now."

So, I was the only one who saw him press the limits of propriety with his free hand under the bar top, and witnessed her flush of excitement at his daring, even if she thought it was a little gross, as well. She didn't drink too much. He didn't try and get her drunk. They talked about politics, bemoaning the state of the world and the people who let it get to this point, raking their eyes over the rest of the bar as though we were at fault.

He played Linh differently than he had Regina, honing in on the small things that made her feel like he cared, like he was the only one who truly understood her. His attention was that of a lover, the perfect friend, except twisted so that once he screwed himself into your life, removing him would rip out most of your vital organs in the process. But even if Linh recognized that, the allure of his unconditional (for now) approval was too much to resist. She could say no at any point, she surely told herself. She could quit anytime she wanted to.

Linh was a biology teacher at Lanier Middle School. Had been a biology teacher, I should say, because her leaving school was what began this downward spiral. She'd always dreamed of teaching science, but she only lasted three years before the focus on testing and state-approved textbooks, fighting among administration and teachers, and arguments with parents unhappy with their child's grades all finally got to her. Linh grew up in a large family in the new Little Saigon on the West side of town, every adult pushing their kids to get a great education, all the kids studying hard for the teachers who were venerated as saints. Now Linh babysat the kids of her brothers and sisters to make ends meet, lived at home with her parents, and couldn't escape their disappointment over her failure. Instead of trying for another teaching job, she returned to her second love, painting. In her room at night, she sketched out the landscapes of her dreams in watercolors, then hid the finished paintings in her closet behind all of her abandoned teacher wear.

Near midnight, pleasantly aglow, Linh left with George, her carefully spiked hair mussed from his hand running through it, her leather jacket thrown over his shoulder. At the swinging front doors, just after kicking them open with her worn Doc Martens, she glanced back. Her eyes skated over everything else like she was sketching the scene in her brain.

I never saw Linh again. The regulars figured she'd moved out to San Francisco like she'd always wanted to, or followed her friend Brittany to Portland.

But two days after leaving with Linh, George returned with his I-don't-care-if-you-ignore-me grin, his skin smooth and his hair sleek. He was just as trim as always, his face a narrow blade, and he sat like a contented cat who'd done something it knew it shouldn't have done but doesn't regret it. George left large tips, but the bartenders gave those dollars back to other customers as soon as they could, using the money as change. They always washed their hands.

What was wrong with George? That was the question no one seemed to be able to answer. He smelled slightly off, one woman would say. A group of guys claimed that when he played pinball, he talked to the machine like it was an ex. The bar as a whole decided George was just *wrong*, the generic definition of it.

I knew what the problem was. He was trying too hard, and if you try too hard to fit in then you never will.

But the women George brought to Poison Girl never knew him long enough to spot his personality straining at the seams. One-night stands, all of them, even the ones who'd been hanging out in the bar long enough to know *of* him. He starts talking to them and they think, "Oh, he's different than everyone said," and, "Maybe I've just never given him a chance." They're fascinated by how he watches their face and lips, actually listening to what they say. And then they go out that door and never come back.

Rani was a tattoo artist from the east side of Houston who came to Poison Girl to drink outside of her neighborhood. She stayed away from all the local tattoo artists because she didn't want drama, and because she didn't want to start trouble with her ex and her son's father, who was a tattoo artist as well and insanely jealous. In each of her designs, she'd leave a piece of herself, a bit of what she'd seen that day. A shriveled leaf. A cicada shell. Every Sunday, she'd call her father and talk for hours, since he was taking care of her mother who was in the throes of early-onset Alzheimer's.

Kaylee worked the front of a high-end restaurant in River Oaks. Her hometown was out in West Texas, a city she never named because she was sure no one would recognize it. She left her family and her past behind, but you could see who she was in the fragility of her smile and the way she lingered on the last letter when writing down a name on the waitlist. Two younger sisters were back in that city she never named, and she drank her fears for them away when she could, because she couldn't do anything else.

Jillisa ran fundraising for a local politician. She also took care of their social media accounts, which meant when she walked into Poison Girl at the end of the day, she folded her thin body up onto a bar stool like winter clothing being packed away for the summer. Every vile reply she'd read, every outburst of hatred, it poured back out of her in the way she ripped the cardboard beer coasters into smaller and smaller shreds.

Harriet took no shit from anyone and gave shit only to those who deserved it.

Margarita only drank her namesake, which she saw as something of a penance for being a bartender with a drink for a name.

Wendy tipped the homeless man outside the bar's entrance both on the way in and on the way out. Because she was generous or forgetful, no one ever knew.

After they left with George, we never saw them again.

George was good at picking out women who the world outside Poison Girl's doors wouldn't miss. But Poison Girl missed those women, even if the regulars believed they'd all found better lives or more exciting jobs rather than something worse. No one wanted to jump to conclusions. No one wanted to worry. But I knew they were gone *and* who they'd gone with.

It was incredibly easy to turn myself into the kind of woman who attracted George's ever-roving eye. He didn't have a physical type so much as an aura, and with a little extra eyeliner and a messy unraveling of my braided hair, I made myself into the me who'd attract a man like him.

When he walked into the bar that night, his eyes locked on me so immediately he stumbled over a couple putting away their IDs. He'd let his hunger take control. What he usually kept tightly leashed was apparent from his every movement like the smell of rotten meat. He dropped into the seat next to me, and that was the first time since he opened the door to the bar that I looked directly at him.

"I've never seen you in here before," he said. "With your beauty, I certainly would've noticed."

I nodded, but it wasn't my beauty he noticed. Now that he was close, he read what kind of woman I was, how best to get inside my defenses. He waved a hand at Ricky who gave me a look, asking if I wanted him to run the guy off, but I shook my head.

"A Willett for the lady, neat."

His instincts weren't all wrong.

I touched his shoulder. "I couldn't, really."

"I insist," he said.

Ricky brought him a Lone Star and set the Willett before me. I took a sip, but it did nothing to alleviate my thirst. We chatted about the bar, and he pretended to be friends with everyone in there because he must have suspected being social was more likely to get me to open up. He told me what I already knew about the bar, the neighborhood, and when he started in about the disco ball and how it had been up there for ten straight years, when in fact it was only recently hung, I interrupted him.

"You're doing this all wrong."

"What?" he said, a slur that wasn't from the beer evident in his voice.

"You're too obvious. You pick on the walking wounded but don't act wounded yourself. You're playacting rather than being."

His eyes sharpened. This wasn't the way he wanted this to go, but he was too confident to second-guess himself. "Another Willett?"

"You know that's not what I'm here for."

My hand on his thigh set his body into motion. He leaned forward and pulled me toward him with a hand on my waist. A long, thin knife appeared in his other hand, glittering in the dim light, nearly pressing against my stomach, but I regained my stool with a small, embarrassed laugh, acting as if I hadn't seen it.

"Not here," I whispered.

His fever-bright eyes shrank to pinpricks as he pulled himself together, his knees so weak I had to hold him up as I led him to a dark corner in the back of the bar where we could stand together and look like we were making out.

And though I was starving for it—the hunger he couldn't control raging through me as well—I put my hands to either side of his head and whispered in his ear, "You should've taken those who prey on their own, you idiot. Those who nobody'll miss because no one ever liked them. The ones everyone's glad to see gone."

Only at that moment did he realize that we were the same kind of monster.

Too late, he noticed the small knife in my own hand, too late the blade entering his neck and piercing his throat. At the same time, I stepped into his arms to prevent him from stabbing me in return. His lips tasted of iron and rotting meat. He had no breath to cry out.

Gently, one arm around his neck and one cradling his waist, I led him out onto the empty back patio in the awkward waltz of eager lovers. With the knife still in the wound, blood only dribbled out. His eyes, oh his intense chameleon eyes, their pupils opened wide, invited me in.

There's a trick to opening the back gate to the dumpsters. Ricky taught me once after the bar closed. Ricky was also the reason I knew the dumpsters would be picked up the next day.

I heaved George's weight in, took back my knife, and watched him disappear just like all those women he took home. I tidied my lipstick, checked my red dress for bloodstains, and left the trash out with the trash.

Ricky raised an eyebrow when I returned to my seat at the bar sans George.

"George got a call about a dying relative," I told him. "It was an emergency, he said. He had to go."

Ricky poured shots of whiskey for himself and me. "To George having had to go."

We toasted and downed the shots.

And, with just a little more whiskey to aid in the forgetting, George'll never be missed.

THE VESSEL

CALEB STEPHENS

I LOVE THE forest. I always have.

I live for the hour I'm allowed outside of the Haven each day, free to gather wildflowers and run through the woods. Mother says I'm much too old for childish things and maybe I am. I'll be fifteen in a week—a woman, according to her—and my days will no longer be my own; they will belong to the Family. I'll do The Work and all that it requires, and the forest will become a memory.

These were my thoughts until yesterday, when I was named the Vessel.

I am going to die tomorrow.

Tonight, I run.

Mother rushes ahead of me, glancing back every few steps to make sure I'm following. Her eyes shine with fear in the moonlight. The same fear pumps hot through my blood with every beat of my heart, every racing breath. What I'm doing is forbidden. The Vessel *never* runs.

The thought fills me with a fresh wave of terror, and I don't see the log until it collides with my shin. My teeth rattle as I crash down, splinters of pain tearing through my ribs. But Mother's hands seize my wrists before I can cry out. Her arms heave me back to my feet.

When she speaks, her voice trembles. "Hurry! You know what they'll do if they catch us!"

And I do. My entire life has revolved around the Transcension. The Family has prepared me for this very moment. To be named the Vessel is the *greatest* honor the Family can give one of its children. All my life I've been told that sacrifice is the ultimate form of love, that to give my life for the Family is pure joy.

But I don't feel joy as Mother pulls me forward. All I feel is terror because I can hear them chasing us now. Their voices roar for my return, their cries arrowing through the trees like living things.

Go, I think, *run!*

I do. Mother moves with a speed I've never seen before. She's always been a woman of precise movement. A woman whose authority is felt rather than heard. But the way she charges through the woods without care or concern fills me with an indescribable amount of fear, and not for myself as much as for her. Mine will be a peaceful death, both honorable and just.

Mother's will not. If she is captured, she will burn.

Stars flash overhead in handfuls of glitter. The trees slip past like skeletons, their branches white with moonlight. My shin throbs with the fresh ache of a new bruise, but I ignore the pain. I must push on for Mother because she is doing the same for me. Our fates are linked—we can't be caught. I don't know where we are or where we're going, only that I've never gone this deep into the forest before. To wander this far from the Haven is forbidden—it puts everyone in the Family at risk. Outsiders roam these hills, and they are not to be trusted.

My entire being hums with this terrible knowledge. It would swallow me whole if it weren't for Mother. She casts a nervous glance back at me, but I can tell she has a plan. She's moving with purpose, like she has a destination in mind. She's always done that for me. My entire life she's been my compass, my guiding light. And not just for me—for the Family. Her words carry weight. Everyone understands this.

Everyone but Brother Abel.

Lately, I've seen him whispering with Brother Winslow while tossing hateful looks at Mother, his eyebrows slanting down when she speaks. It's different from the way he looks at me. His eyes are like two little mouths always trying to drink me in. I hate his eyes, but I hate his voice worse. And it's his voice rising behind me now, coming closer.

"Get back here, you little bitch!"

The fine hairs on the back of my neck rise. My lungs stitch with pain. Every breath is a war. I've been running for hours now, or what *feels* like hours, trying to keep pace with Mother as she bulls through the brush. Branches scrape my arms. Piles of deadfall assault my legs and calves, bare beneath my nightgown. I didn't have a chance to change when Mother woke me with a hand over my mouth and a whisper in my ear.

"It's time. We must go now!"

No one saw us leave. I was certain of it, yet the footsteps crash closer behind us, and closer still. Ahead, Mother pauses, waiting for me to catch up.

"Mother, watch out!" I cry when I see the shadow streaking downslope through the trees.

She snaps her head left an instant before she's swallowed by a pair of muscular arms and driven to the ground. I open my mouth to scream, only to taste sour sweat and dirty skin as a hand clamps over my mouth. Hot breath hits my ear in an angry hiss.

"You little cunt, you didn't really think you'd get away from us, did you?" Brother Abel asks. He wrenches my arm behind my back and drives me forward with painful force, stopping near Mother, who's pinned to the ground beneath Brother Winslow. He's several years younger than Brother Abel with the face of a weasel and a smile that fills my veins with ice. Two more figures slip from the trees behind him, and it takes a moment for their features to materialize. When they do, my stomach drops: It's the twins. Ian and Kelsey, my best friends. I tell them everything, trust them with my secrets. And I did this very afternoon when I told them I was leaving. I had to say goodbye.

But they betrayed me. And now all I can think is *why?*

Kelsey reads the hurt in my face and glances away. "Don't look at me like that," she says. "You know leaving like this isn't—"

"Fair," Ian finishes. "You were chosen as the Vessel. The Orator never lies."

"No, he doesn't," Brother Winslow says, his thin lips curling into a sneer.

Mother doesn't look at him, stares only at Brother Abel with her dark eyes washed in starlight. "You will let her go. You know my word is law."

He barks a laugh as his fingers dig deeper into my cheeks. "You think you can still give us orders after this? After everything you've just—"

I sink my teeth deep into the meat of his palm and bite. Blood erupts along with a shout that quickly turns to a roar—and I am free. I fly toward Brother Winslow and hurl myself at him. I must save Mother just as she tried to save me.

We hit the turf together, and I transform into a whirlwind of fingernails and gnashing teeth.

Scratching. Biting.

Clawing at his eyes.

Tearing at his ears, nose, mouth, powered by a single, blazing thought—the only thing that matters.

He. Will. Not. Hurt. Mother.

And then the twins are on me, dragging me back, pulling me away. Brother Winslow scowls and takes his feet with a razor-blade smile slicing across his chin. He tuts and shakes his head, then retrieves a rock from the ground. "Well now, little one, that was stupid."

"You will not touch her!" Mother cries.

"Shut your mouth!" The bright smack of flesh hitting flesh fills the air, and I realize Brother Abel has done the unthinkable. He has *slapped* Mother. She is never, *ever*, to be hit. She is divine, sacred above all else. He yanks her back by the hair, laughing as she struggles to reach me, his eyes on Brother Winslow.

"Do it. Kill the girl."

My blood turns to ice. Brother Winslow steps closer and raises the rock. Kelsey and Ian tighten their grip on my arms, and I know I won't see another sunrise. My eyes lock with Mother's and I mouth, *I'm sorry.* And I am. She is everything to me, My entire world. And she will burn because I betrayed her trust. They will make her suffer because of *me.*

I close my eyes and brace for the blow…and then open them when it doesn't come.

All around me, halos of light bleed through the branches, tongues of flame drawing closer.

Fireflies, I think. And then: *No, torches.*

The closest peels from the trees, and I recognize the sallow, skin-stretched face and hollow cheeks of the Orator. "Let go of the rock," he orders in a voice barely above a whisper, but Brother Winslow already has, backing away from me with his hands raised, as are the twins.

The Orator levels his cold gaze on Brother Abel. "Release her."

"No. Come any closer, and I break her neck."

He will. I see the truth of the statement in the way his arm cinches tighter beneath Mother's chin, the way his jaw hardens.

"If you do," the Orator hisses, "we will strip your skin."

Members of the Family step from the trees and encircle us, so many I wonder if even the elders came. Brother Abel holds the Orator's gaze a moment longer—defiance flickering in his eyes, covering his fear—until, with a long exhalation, he loosens his grip. The instant he does, two men seize him.

Mother rushes toward me and brushes the pine needles from my clothes. "Are you okay, my darling?"

I nod, my cheeks slick with tears. I am. *Somehow.* "Are you?"

She smiles, her face the picture of serenity, her long, dark hair sweeping low over her shoulders. "Yes. We were never truly in danger." She surveys Brother Abel and Brother Winslow, and her eyes harden. "But they are. Bring them."

She takes my hand and leads me back into the forest. The Family follows. We walk in silence, and I wonder why we aren't returning to the Haven when Mother angles further upslope and pushes deeper into the woods. I want to ask her, but I've been taught to never question her decisions, to never doubt, only to follow.

So, I do.

After a time, the trees thin and the sky blushes with peach light. Mother guides me through a clearing of waist-high grass toward the sound of the ocean. The smell of salt fills my nose, and a cool breeze drifts over my skin. We reach a bluff, and I catch sight of waves crashing far below, pulling back and slamming forward again in ceaseless motion. I've never seen the ocean before. It's beautiful. *The* most beautiful thing I've ever seen. But I can't sink into the moment like I want to. Something feels…off.

Tendrils of dread snake down my spine when my assailants are directed toward the edge of the cliff and placed in a line. Behind them, the sun rises in a golden orb, and despite the warmth, a chill runs through me. The twins seem to feel it too, their eyes flooding with terror at the great height. They turn and plead with Mother to forgive them. They're sorry, they say. Brother Abel forced them to do this, and it wasn't their fault. Brother Winslow says the same, but Mother gazes at the horizon and says nothing. She looks peaceful once more. She looks *right.*

Brother Abel looks anything but, his eyes cold pools of hate, his lips pulled tight. I would fear for Mother's safety if it weren't for Brother Paul standing next to him, holding him in place. That man is the tallest in the Family by a foot, with palms the size of dinner plates and fingers as thick as sausages. Brother Abel will never escape.

"Brother Abel," Mother says, shifting her gaze his way, "you have been found guilty of treason."

"*You* are guilty of treason!" he spits back before Mother can continue. "You fled with the Vessel!"

She sighs and shakes her head. "Tell me, Brother Abel, why is it that, after sowing so much discord among my flock, you could only convince these few to pursue me?"

He blanches, but his anger remains, still simmering in the sharp lines of his face. "Because these *few* are the only true believers. The Vessel shall never flee! It is the *law.*"

Her eyes narrow. "*I* am the law! And I've long suspected your disloyalty. All I needed was to give you a reason to act." She regards the twins, and then turns toward me with a tender look of hurt—and I suddenly know why.

"*We leave tonight,*" she'd said after I'd been named the Vessel. "*Tell no one.*"

And I hadn't. Only the twins. Mother knew I would, but how could I not? We grew up together, after all. They were like siblings to me, and I couldn't bear to leave them without saying goodbye. But Mother never trusted the twins. She'd told me time and time again they didn't have my best interests at heart. Brother Abel raised them, after all, so they came from bad stock. I disagreed. I said they were my friends. My *best* friends. "*They're jealous, petty creatures,*" she'd replied. "*They'll betray you the first chance they get.*"

And they had.

I can't bear to look at Mother any longer, so I hang my head as the Orator steps forward and sets his pale hand on Brother Abel's chest. Brother Abel's jaw twitches with fear, but he doesn't break, doesn't crumble, just stares at the man with contempt, his hands bound behind his back.

The Orator returns his gaze, his pale, bald head shining in the morning sun. "You have conspired against the Family. For the crimes of blasphemy and treason against our Holy Mother, you have sacrificed paradise. I cast you out!" He shoves Brother Abel, and he flies from view without a sound, swallowed by the cool morning air. A gasp ripples through the Family. I feel like I might faint.

The Orator turns his attention to Brother Winslow, who is now weeping in fear, held in place by Brother Jacob and Brother Elias. His calculating grin has long since faded, beads of sweat breaking over his forehead, which shines like wax. "Take pity on me, Mother," he pleads. "Forgive me for I have sinned."

Mother gives him a sorrowful smile. "Your sins are forgiven, Brother Winslow. You will be with us on The Day of Ascension."

Brother Winslow exhales in relief, the terror flushing from his narrow face.

"But you still must face the consequences of what you have done." Mother nods at the Orator.

Brother Winslow shakes his head as the Orator approaches. "Oh, God, no. Please, no. Don't do this. You don't have to do this!"

"Oh, but I do," the Orator says before he shoves.

The twins scream. The ocean thunders and roars.

The twins cry and, despite their betrayal, I can't bring myself to hate them. But I can't stop what is about to happen. All I can do is pray that Mother grants them mercy and gives them another chance.

She slides in front of them with her hands clasped at her waist. "My children, you have broken the law. You have sinned against your elders. And you have sinned against me. Do you admit your guilt? Will you repent?"

Kelsey blinks and wipes her eyes. "Yes, Mother. Forgive us."

"Yes, Mother," Ian says, his gaze tilting toward his feet.

"I appreciate your penitence. But you have also betrayed my daughter," Mother continues, looking my way for an instant. "You sought to bring her harm."

Ian straightens. "No. It was our father's command. We're taught to obey our elders."

"You are to obey your father, yes. But you also broke the trust of someone close to you and revealed your true character. And not just anyone, but my daughter."

"But she was chosen!" Kelsey screeches. "She was named the Vessel. And she fled!"

"Yes, but who did she flee with?"

Kelsey swallows. "You, Mother."

"Correct. Me. And would I ever do anything to hurt the Family?"

"No, Mother." A tear drips from Kelsey's chin. She lowers her gaze. "Never. Please forgive me."

Mother places a finger beneath her chin and tilts her eyes higher, a smile breaking across her face. "I believe you. And I forgive you. But you must atone if your soul is to join ours on the Day of Ascension. Bless you, child." And then, with a quick snap of her wrist, Kelsey is gone. Ian cries out and lunges for Mother, but the Orator intercepts him and sends him flying backward into open air. His screams fade and then snuff out.

No. It's all I can think as my eyes burn and tears leak down my face. *They're gone—both of them are gone.* I'm still crying when

Mother pulls me into a hug and pats my back. She smells like she always does—fresh leaves. Flowers and rain.

"It's okay, my darling. It's over."

"*Why?*" I ask, though I know it's forbidden to question Mother. Her actions are infallible. She is the voice of the Creator.

"What I did, I did for them. Their souls were soiled. This was the only way they could join us in paradise. Come." She laces her fingers through mine and pulls me forward toward the edge of the cliff. There, I peer down, terrified I will see the bodies of my friends, or those of the men who tried to harm me, but all I see are waves capped in seams of foam. All I hear is the boom and hiss of the sea.

Mother thumbs a tear from my cheek. "Don't mourn them. Your friends aren't gone. They're still with us. They're in the water and in the air. They're in our hearts. Their energy is *everywhere*. Close your eyes and you'll feel them. You'll sense how they've been set free."

I do as I'm told. I breathe. I smell sea salt and the sweet, sharp scent of the grass rising from beneath my feet. The rising sun bathes my skin in a pleasant warmth. But I don't sense Kelsey and Ian as Mother says I will. All I feel is grief.

"You can perceive them, yes?" Mother asks.

"Yes," I lie. I open my eyes and realize Mother is no longer at my side. She's standing behind me now, next to the Orator. I shiver beneath his gaze as I turn. His eyes have always unnerved me, the whites tinged a pale pink, the irises the blue of frozen ice. They hold me in place as the Family presses closer.

"What…what are you doing, Mother?" I ask.

"You know what must happen."

A chill ripples down my arms. I do know, but I can't believe it. Every member of the Family calls her Mother, but I'm the only one able to do so by blood. She's always told me I'm special, that I'm different from the others. It's why she fled with me, why she was willing to sacrifice the Family to keep me alive.

Except she wasn't.

Her eyes gloss with tears as Brother Felix begins the Reaping song. His full-throated voice fills the air. The Family joins in.

I can see them all so clearly in the morning sun: Sister Alice with her butter-yellow hair pulled into a braid; Brother Sirus, my elementary teacher, with his bald head and thick beard; Brother Colton, the blacksmith and his wife Sister Grace; and Sister Hannah and Clarice, my choir instructors, singing without much fervor, tears creasing their face. Every one of these people have formed me, have made me who I am. And each of them will now stand here and watch me die.

My tears spot the toes of my shoes as Mother pulls me into an embrace. Her arms tighten and she kisses the tears from my cheek like she did when I was just a little girl, waking from a nightmare. *It's not real, darling. Mother's here.*

But this *is* real. I am the Vessel, the embodiment of the Family's sin—a sacrifice to the Creator in hopes he will bless the Family with another bountiful harvest and a year of good fortune and health.

Mother pulls back and wipes her tears, and I realize she is not without feeling, that she *has* always loved me and is just doing what she must. "Don't fear what is to come," she says. "The life we're sending you to is a beautiful one."

A million questions run through my head at this, but the only one that comes out is, "But who will replace you when you're gone? Who will be the new mother?"

She hesitates, and her hand slides lower in a motion I nearly miss, her palm running over the soft curve of her belly. The Orator places his hand on hers and Mother gives me a sad smile—one full of both joy and hurt. "The Creator has been kind to us. Your sister will carry on. Her name will be Quinn."

A baby, I think. *She's going to have a baby. I've been replaced.*

And it's with that thought that Mother sets her hand on my chest—and I take flight.

TREAT DAY

J. E. ROWNEY

"YOU LOVE THE aquarium," he tells me.

I must have mentioned it once, maybe back when we first met, and it's stuck in his head. My husband does that, remembers all the little details. I swear sometimes I almost suspect that he writes things down, keeps a log of everything I ever say. I'm careful with my words, just in case.

"Thank you."

I smile, because it's the polite thing to do.

It's not like I'm going to start an argument about this. I'm sure he doesn't want to either, despite what you might think. Today is Treat Day. That's how it works. Yesterday was yesterday, and today is Treat Day. I've paid for it, so I might as well try to enjoy it. I have to look like I'm enjoying it, anyway.

"You'll want to cover that up," he says, pointing to the bruise, even though he doesn't need to.

I nod. I don't have any words yet. Sometimes it's best to say nothing.

I do what he says, and stare at myself for a split second too long while I'm looking in the bathroom mirror.

"Little Miss Vain." He smiles, sidling up behind me, wrapping his arms around me, kissing the top of my head. "Look at you. Still pretty, aren't you? Still pretty."

He gets another smile, and I turn my head around, turn my body around, press my face into his chest.

His hands are firm against my back as he embraces me. I can feel the size of them, spread across my ribcage. I can also feel that I am shaking, and I will myself to stop.

"Ready?" he asks, as he finally lets go. "It's already late. What time does it close? Three? Four?"

He has planned this, not I. I haven't the first idea, but I have to answer.

"Four," my mouse-squeak voice offers.

"You don't sound too sure about that. Four, is it?"

I try to sound certain in my uncertainty. "Four."

He looks at me just long enough to make my palms start to sweat, and that heavy sick feeling nudges at my gut, but then he smiles and strokes my cheek.

"Four. Okay," he says, and nods towards the door.

I sit quietly in the car, and when we arrive, I remain seated until he walks around to my door and opens it for me. He likes to do that, make a show of being gentlemanly. When we first started dating, it impressed me, as I'm sure it was designed to do. Now I feel obligated to stay in the passenger seat until he lets me out.

"There you go, sweetheart," he says, reaching for my hand.

"Thank you," I say, because it's the polite thing to do.

His hand is cold, almost inhumanly so. It feels as though I'm holding onto a flabby piece of meat rather than my husband. My fingers are squashed together, the band on my ring digging into my flesh. I relax against the pain and quicken my step to keep pace with him.

The first thing he asks, when we get to the front desk: What time does this place close?

Four.

He looks at me, and I'm not sure whether there's disappointment or pride tucked away in his expression.

It doesn't give us long. Treat Day used to be Treat Week. Sometimes it was even longer. Today, it's a few hours in the afternoon after a night that spread itself into the day. I'm not tired though, not really. If I let myself feel tired, my attention will drift, and I'll lose focus. I can't do that.

He pays for the tickets and pulls me in, close to his side. When he kisses the top of my head again, the woman behind the counter smiles at me. I'm a lucky girl. He is such a good man. So, I smile back, because it's the polite thing to do. All these responses that I have learned to give. Such a good girl. I really am.

He starts to lead me, following the line of arrows on the floor. This direction, this way around. It's all laid out for us; all we have to do is comply and we'll get to see everything.

It's not bad. There are turtles and jellyfish and sharks and fish, fish, fish. He walks; I walk beside him. He's taller than I, and faster. Stronger too, but that doesn't matter so much today, or at least not right now. Every so often he leans to peer into a tank or read the tiny rectangular sign next to an exhibit, and I stop, and I read, and I wait.

"Do you like it?" he asks but doesn't pause for an answer. "It's okay, isn't it?"

It feels like a trap. Do I agree it's okay or do I say it's wonderful?

"Thank you for bringing me," I say, trying not to stumble.

He looks at me, as if thinking about something, and then smiles.

"Sure," he says. "What you want, you get. You always do. Everything you want. Isn't that right?"

We are standing in front of a floor-to-ceiling tank. An octopus is lazily spreading one leg out toward the glass.

"You…" I stop to think about my words. "Thank you," I say, more quietly this time.

He tightens his grip on my hand still further, his fingers spreading like the octopus's tentacles, reaching my wrist. He presses gently, almost innocently onto the place hidden beneath my sleeve where my pink flesh has turned mottled purple. I breathe. I keep still. I don't recoil. I wonder if an octopus's tentacles grow back if they are cut off. I wonder if I could snap my arm off, let it go, and run away. I wouldn't care about it growing back. I wouldn't care about leaving it here, attached to him instead of me, lost forever.

"It's your day, sweetheart," he says, without a shred of emotion.

The pain thuds in my wrist, and I smile. My face throbs, and I smile. I want to vomit, and I smile.

And so, we go on.

Room after room, all the same. Tanks, more tanks. All kinds of creatures separated from us by glass and water. The brave or brazen watch us watching them; the timid hide behind rocks or dart into greenery. I stand by his side; I used to love the aquarium.

We get to the end well before four. I wish for more rooms, more of the same, more tanks, more fish, more time. Better here than at home.

In the last room before the gift shop, he looks down at me.

"I need to hit the men's room before we go," he says. "You stay there. Don't move. Don't talk to anyone."

I nod.

"You know what will happen," he says. It's not a question, it's a statement, and it is true.

I nod again.

His mouth is almost touching my ear, his breath hot upon my skin.

"Good girl." Straightening up, he reaches down and strokes my hair, so softly, so gently.

I remember when it felt good, or at least I almost remember. It's like catching sight of something in your peripheral vision: You know it's there, but you can't quite see it when you try to look again.

He walks away. I freeze. The tank reflects his departing figure. My heart races. I count the seconds.

There's a huge fish, pale, fat and ugly, suspended behind the glass. The tank looks too small for such a massive creature, but he probably doesn't notice. They have poor memories, don't they, fish? By the time he swims to one side of the tank he'll have forgotten how far he's gone. He'll have forgotten how long he has been in there, caught within the glass walls, recycling the same dark water through his gills, repeating the same actions on an endless loop. Swim. Eat. Breathe. It's not a bad life. Is it?

There's a child, a toddler, maybe four or five years old, zooming around the room while the mother stands, leaning against the wall, yapping into her mobile phone. He—no, I think it's a she—has her arms out like an airplane, or at least that's what I think at first.

The more I watch her, the reality dawns on me that she's trying to mimic some kind of fish fins, moving her mouth in a goldfish "O." She catches my eye, and I look away. I don't want her to think I'm that weird stranger that watches kids and run screaming to her mum and pointing at me. If he came back and saw…

The fish-girl runs to the tank and presses her face up to the glass. That's almost enough to make me say something. The dirt, the germs, her little face. I snap a look over to the mother, but she's turned the opposite direction.

"Hey." I say it too quietly. I can barely hear my own voice.

Thud, thud, thud. Her tiny fists pound against the tank wall.

The huge fish moves more quickly than I would ever have expected. I thought it would be like an ocean liner, slowly maneuvering itself around, shifting its heavy body through the water as though it were swimming through tar. Instead, it almost darts. An initial shocked judder and then a flicked movement to shift it in the opposite direction, away from the danger.

"Hey!" Louder this time. "Stop that."

The volume of my words startles me.

I turn and look toward the mother, look toward the bathroom. It's okay. Everything is okay.

"Stop that," I repeat.

The kid stares at me in round-mouthed surprise. She looks over at the mother and makes the first movements of speech.

I put my finger on my lips, and with the other hand, I make a beckoning gesture. Come here, come here, quiet now.

Not taking her eyes off the mother, the child slowly moves toward me.

"You shouldn't do that," I say. Stern but quiet. Not attracting any attention.

The girl says nothing. She stands in front of me, so close that she could reach out and touch me, and she says nothing. Instead, she runs her eyes over my face, and her expression changes from fear of reprehension to morbid curiosity.

And now I don't care about the fish. I don't care about the noise of the kid and the banging on the glass and how unfair it is that an animal can be kept like that in a tank that's too small, too constraining, too numbingly boring. It doesn't matter.

We stare at each other, the child and I, without words, until she reaches her hand forward, and brings her fingers close, so close. I think she's going to touch me, I'm almost sure of it, but she doesn't. She stops a whisker's breadth away, her hand suspended in the air between us.

Breathe. Breathe steadily, keep it slow. Pretend you have gills, filtering the feelings out. Let it go.

My eyes are locked on her face, but hers are wandering over mine.

"Sophie." The word doesn't have any effect. It might as well be in a different room, a different city, a different universe. Under water.

"Sophie." The mother reaches down, jerks at the girl's wrist. "I'm so sor—" She starts to apologize to me, this suit-and-heels woman. Probably left work early to catch the school run. No one dresses like this for fun. She starts to apologize, but then she sees what Sophie saw.

"Come away, Sophie." She straightens herself and tugs at the child's arm.

The child whose name is Sophie is still looking at me, spellbound, stuck in the moment. Before the mother can drag her away, she brings her unrestrained hand up to her sticky mouth, kisses her fingers and pushes them forward toward my face.

Before they can make contact, the mother gives a yank, scoops the child up onto her hip. She stares at me for a split second before walking rapidly to the exit, her heels clacking on the tiled floor. It's not a look of pity, it's not solidarity, it's disgust.

And then I am alone. He isn't back, and for that I am thankful. He didn't see what happened. There's no one to tell him. Just me and the fish. Alone.

I want to get up, to walk over to the tank and look into the blackness, see if I can see the fish. There's no sign of him now, not since the banging. It's a too-small tank, but it's dark, there's still room enough to float to the back and try to hide.

I sit on the slab bench, staring forward, trying to catch some trace of the fish, but there's nothing. All I can see is my own reflection.

The sound of approaching footsteps makes my heart race. He'll be back from the bathroom any moment. I stand up, drawn to the tank as if by an invisible force. My fingers reach out, touching the cool glass. The huge fish emerges from the shadows, its eyes level with mine.

In that moment, I see myself reflected in its dark, ancient gaze. We're both trapped, both suffocating in spaces too small for us. But unlike me, this fish never knew freedom. It doesn't know there's a whole ocean out there.

I do.

A throat clears behind me. I don't turn around immediately. Instead, I press my palm flat against the glass, a silent promise to the fish and to myself.

"What are you doing?" His voice is calm, but I can hear the underlying tension.

I take a deep breath and turn to face him. For the first time in years, I meet his gaze squarely. "I think," I say, my voice barely above a whisper but steady, "I'd like to go home now."

His eyebrows raise slightly at my direct response. "Of course, sweetheart. Whatever you want."

As we walk towards the exit, I catch the eye of a woman entering with her teenage daughter. Something in my expression makes her pause. She looks from me to my husband, a flicker of concern crossing her face. I give her the smallest of nods.

It's a tiny gesture, imperceptible to him. But to me, it feels monumental. For the first time in years, I've acknowledged my situation to someone else. As we step out into the fading afternoon light, I realize that I may be trapped for now, but I still remember what freedom tastes like.

And for the first time in a long time, I allow myself to hope.

ABOUT THE AUTHORS

Sam Brackett has always been fascinated by all things dark and spooky. When he's not reading or writing, you can find him out on a run or haunting a local brewery. Though his heart remains in Vermont, his home for nearly a decade, Sam currently lives in Florida, where swampy horrors never cease.

Mia Dalia is an internationally published, CWA-nominated author of all things fantastic, thrilling, scary, and strange. Her short stories have been featured in a variety of anthologies, magazines, literary journals, and narrative podcasts, and have been voted into the top ten of *Tales to Terrify* 2023 and short-listed for the CWA's Daggers Awards 2024. She is the author of the novels *Estate Sale* and *Haven;* novellas *Alakazam, Tell Me a Story, Discordant, Arrokoth,* and *Do You Know The Muffin Man?;* and the collection *Smile So Red and Other Tales of Madness.* Visit daliaverse.wixsite.com/author to learn more.

Cat Delani is a horror writer living in Annapolis, MD. When she isn't writing, you can find her reading endless books and, recently, cheering on Cleveland sports. *Unclaimed Property* is her first novella. Visit catdelani.com to learn more.

Christopher O'Halloran is the factory-working Canadian actor-turned-author of *Pushing Daisy,* his debut novel from Lethe Press. His shorter work has been published or is forthcoming from *Uncharted, Kaleidotrope, NoSleep Podcast, Cosmic Horror Monthly, Brigid's Gate, Dark Moon Books,* and others, and he is the editor of the anthology *Howls from the Wreckage.* Visit coauthor.ca to learn more.

Alex Hoeft is an award-winning news reporter covering the Lake Tahoe region in California and Nevada. When she's not writing for work or fun, she's wrangling her toddler or reading a book, or doing both at the same time. Visit ahoeft.com to learn more.

Frances Hope is a thriller, horror, and mystery writer living in Greater Boston. As a young child growing up in the San Francisco Bay Area, she loved writing disturbing horror fiction—when she wasn't obsessively rereading her favorite book on how to be a kid detective. Fine her online at franceshope.com.

Jade Jiao is a British author working primarily in scripts and short stories. In 2024, she was a quarter-finalist in the Killer Shorts Screenplay Competition, and her short story "Wilful" was featured in Speculation Publication's *Grimm Retold* anthology. She has upcoming stories set to appear in *The Thin Veil Press*, *Chthonic Matter Quarterly*, and *Borderline Tales*.

Nick Kolakowski is the author of several horror and crime novels, including *Where the Bones Lie* (Datura Books) and *Love & Bullets* (Shotgun Honey). His short stories and nonfiction essays have appeared in various anthologies and magazines, including *CrimeReads*, *Mystery Magazine*, *Dark Yonder*, and more. He lives and writes in New York City.

Andrew Kozma's fiction appears in *Apex*, *Factor Four*, and *Analog*, while his poems appear in *Strange Horizons*, *The Deadlands*, and *Contemporary Verse 2*. His first book of poems, *City of Regret*, won the Zone 3 First Book Award, and his second book, *Orphanotrophia*, was published in 2021 by Cobalt Press. Visit andrewkozma.net to learn more.

Catlyn Ladd loves alliteration, the sibilant slip of similar sounds. She blends metaphors and archetypes from the shadow self, illuminating the monsters that gestate there. Catlyn worked as a stripper before becoming a professor of philosophy, religion, and women's studies. Her fiction has been published in over a dozen magazines and anthologies, including ones by Black Hare Press, Dark Lit Press, and Skywatcher Press. Her nonfiction book, *Strip: The Making of a Feminist,* is published by Changemakers. Her debut novel *As Those Above Fall* is from Winding Road Stories. She lives with her partner and cats in Colorado. She can be found at www.catlynladd.com.

Amanda Cecelia Lang is is a horror author and aspiring monster-slayer from Colorado. As a die-hard scary movie nerd, her favorite things are meta-slashers, '80s nostalgia, and the rise of a fierce final girl. If she dies after fighting a B-movie monster, she will consider it a good death. Her scary stories currently haunt the dark corners of many popular podcasts, magazines, and anthologies, including *The Deadlands, Gamut, Ghoulish Tales, Cast of Wonders,* and Flame Tree's *Darkness Beckons.* Her short story collection *Saturday Fright at the Movies: 13 Tales from the Multiplex* is available now through Dark Matter INK. You can stalk her work at amandacecelialang.com—just don't be surprised if she leaps out at you from the shadows.

Jessica Lévai has loved stories and storytellers her whole life. After a double major in history and mathematics, a PhD in Egyptology, and eight years of the adjunct shuffle, she devoted herself to writing full-time. You can find her work at *Strange Horizons, Translunar Travelers Lounge,* and *Reactor.* Her first novella, *The Night Library of Sternendach: A Vampire Opera in Verse,* won the Lord Ruthven Award for Fiction. She dreams of one day collaborating on a graphic novel.

Chris McGrane's short stories have appeared in a number of publications, including *Daily Science Fiction.* Chris has received politely worded rejection letters from a number of prominent publishers, literary competitions, and dating agencies.

J. B. McLaurin loves all things Stephen King and John Carpenter. He plays drums in alt-metal band Impossible Machine. His horror-crime novel *Black Echoes* is available from Sley House Publishing. Mobius Blvd. recently published "Covenant," a short story about haunted Halloween decorations, and Undertaker Books featured his story "Passenger" in the *Judicial Homicide Anthology* benefiting death-row inmates later exonerated. His road trip horror tale "Come see the Amazing Holler Owl" is now available from Sley House publishing. Visit jbmclaurinauthor.com to learn more.

Marisca Pichette is a queer author based in Massachusetts. Her work has appeared in *Strange Horizons, Clarkesworld, Vastarien, The Magazine of Fantasy & Science Fiction, Fantasy Magazine, Asimov's, Nightmare Magazine*, and others. Her poetry collection, *Rivers in Your Skin, Sirens in Your Hair,* was a finalist for the Bram Stoker and Elgin Awards. Her first novella, *Every Dark Cloud,* is available from Ghost Orchid Press.

Michael A. Reed is a speculative fiction writer and ironically dyslexic English teacher who has mastered the art of being uncomfortable. He loves to write about ghosts, curses, the bizarre, and the more disturbed corners of the human experience.

Kaleigh Rodgerson is a writer living in Illinois with her three pet parakeets. She has an MA in English from Northern Michigan University and a BA in Criminal Justice. She usually writes science fiction and historical fiction.

L. P. Ring is a writer and teacher from Cork, Ireland. He's been published with Bag of Bones Press, *Chthonic Matter, Mythaxis, Shotgun Honey,* and *Black Beacon,* among others, and has written a detective series featuring the Seoul-based detective Jun-young Choi. He lives in Japan with his wife and a cat, which is always around at mealtimes.

J. E. Rowney is an award-winning British author of domestic and psychological thrillers. Her bestselling novels include *Where No One Can Hear You, The House Sitter,* and *Wish You Were Her.* She writes stories about control, survival, and what happens when the person closest to you becomes the greatest threat. Visit jerowney.com for more information.

Caleb Stephens is an award-winning author writing from Denver, Colorado. His novels include the thrillers *You'll Never Know, If You Lie, The Girls in the Cabin,* and *What Waits Below.* His short fiction has appeared in dozens of publications and podcasts, and his story "The Wallpaper Man" was adapted for film in 2022 by Falconer Film and Media. Visit calebstephensauthor.com to learn more.

Cory Swanson has a masterful collection of guitars, a dog who hates large men, and a lovely family who tolerates his early morning writing habit. One day, he'll retire from teaching music and really make a go of the writing thing. Until then, one can enjoy his occasional short story publications, his novella, *Geminus,* and the sequel novel, *Venus the Monk.* He lives and writes in Northern Colorado.

ABOUT THE EDITORS

Noelle W. Ihli is the *USA Today*-bestselling author of eight thriller-suspense novels. She lives in Idaho with her husband, two sons, and two cats. When she's not plotting her next thriller, she's scaring herself with true-crime documentaries or going for a trail ride in the foothills (with her trusty pepper spray). Visit noellewihli.com to learn more.

Steph Nelson is a thriller author who has also dabbled in horror suspense writing. Her first two publications were short stories published in *Human Monsters: A Horror Anthology*, and *Mother: Tales of Love and Terror*. Both anthologies were finalists for the Bram Stoker Award. Her debut thriller, *The Final Scene*, sold over 10,000 copies in the first two months. She's a lifelong PNW girl who currently lives in Idaho. When she's not working on her next story, she's traveling, doing yoga, thrifting for vintage clothes, or devouring books. Visit stephnelsonauthor.com to learn more.

ABOUT THE COVER ARTIST

Drew Huff is an artist and author of several horror and sci-fi books, including LGBTQ sci-fi novella *Landlocked In Foreign Skin,* cosmic horror novel *The Divine Flesh* (Dark Matter INK), cosmic horror novella *My Name Isn't Paul.* Forthcoming horror novels include *The Exodontists* (Nefarious Bat) and *Run To Beat the Devil.* Drew's short fiction has appeared in numerous anthologies. Visit drewehuff.com to learn more.